That Murray Girl

That Murray Girl

The Story of Madeline Murray Matthews

Mary Matthews Schnettler

NORTH STAR PRESS OF ST. CLOUD, INC.

Cover Art: Diane Anderl

Although the events in this book are historically accurate and true, the names of many of the people outside the Murray and Matthews families have been changed in an effort to respect their privacy.

First Edition: December 1999

Printed in the United States of America
by Versa Press, Inc.,
East Peoria, Illinois.

Published by:
North Star Press of St. Cloud, Inc.
P.O. Box 451
St. Cloud, Minnesota 55320

Contents

Prologue
May 1, 1999

MAMA WOULD BE 103 IN JULY. At eighty-three, she still could add a column of thirty numbers in her head and come up with the right answer on the first try. I remember the Casio calculator I gave her many years ago for her birthday, which she kept on her closet shelf in its original wrapper—just in case she ever needed it. Until she was eighty-five, Mama drove her 1965 Chevy Malibu daily, and then she gave it to one of her grandsons only because she feared she might eventually become a menace on the road. For fifty-four years, Mama was a widow, and she raised five children single-handedly after her husband died unexpectedly at age thirty-seven. She had only a fifth-grade education in a one-room country schoolhouse, but her intelligence was phenomenal. I believe Mama was one of the pioneers in the liberation of women back in 1939, when most women were still confined to their kitchens.

When Will Matthews died in 1937, Mama vowed to support her family in whatever direction God led her. That direction turned out to be in sales — first for a major insurance company, then for the John G. Kinnard Investment Company, and, finally, after age sixty-five, for Avon Cosmetics, where she was a long-time member of the President's Club.

In 1949, Mama flew alone to Boston to see her son Lee graduate third in his class from Harvard Medical School. And then, thirty-two years later, she rejoiced when her grandson graduated with honors from Harvard Law School. She did not attend, but I remember Mama's reaction because she never stopped talking about Mother Teresa, "that tiny, wrinkled-up saint," she called her, who received an honorary doctorate from Harvard that same day to a standing ovation from the thousands of people in Harvard Yard.

One of Mama's greatest joys involved reading hundreds of books about the lives of others, but it never occurred to her to jot down a single word about her own life. Yet her courageous life was an inspiration to many of the people who knew and loved her.

This biographical portrait includes sketches of historical, family and personal events that impacted my mother's life, a life much like a hike through rugged mountains.Uphill and down, around precarious turns in the road, getting lost between perception and reality — traveling on the wings of faith most of the way — even Mama herself was amazed by her determination and success because she often thought of herself as an orphan — "that Murray girl."

Acknowledgments

Not having witnessed my mother's childhood, I found it necessary to seek out information on her early years from various historical sources and from as many of her contemporaries as I could still find. My special thanks go to:

Bob Lommel at the Stearns History Museum, who helped me to find books and old news clippings from as far back as 1899.

A kind young student at St. Cloud State University (name unknown), who assisted me in retrieving editions of the *Minneapolis Star and Tribune*.

Madeline Flynn Mullan of Indio, California, and Ursala Flynn Goebel of Edina, Minnesota, farm neighbors of the Murrays, who sent me their personal reflections on Madeline and the Murray family.

Ed Sinclair of St. Joseph, who shared with me a treasured memory of Madeline in her later childhood.

The pastor of the Church of St. Martin, who allowed me to roam through the locked parish cemetery in search of historical data on the Murray family.

Al Ringsmuth of Waite Park, who e-mailed me an account of his mother's orphan train experience. Rose Ringsmuth came to Minnesota on the same train as my mother and remained her loyal, lifetime friend.

Margaret Studer of St. Cloud, who supplied me with four front-page stories from the *St. Cloud Daily Times* and the *Minneapolis Morning Tribune* on the tragic death of her stepson in 1955.

Sister Nancy Hynes of the College of St. Benedict, who read through an early draft of *That Murray Girl* and offered me helpful suggestions.

Diane Anderl, a talented local artist, who drew the charming, illustrative cover sketch for the book.

My editors, Rita, Corinne, and Seal Dwyer, who encouraged me to finish this story and edited the final draft.

My wonderful and wise husband, Ed, who bore with me when I suffered a foot fracture in a car accident not long ago and offered me good counsel. "Maybe you can't walk, but you can write. Get busy and quit feeling sorry for yourself." Without him, this tribute to my mother would never have been written.

That Murray Girl

Madeline - Age Four

Chapter One

The Journey from Nowhere

DURING THE EARLY MORNING HOURS of October 29, 1899, Michael and Rosanna Murray hurried through the remnants of an early Minnesota snowstorm toward the city of St. Cloud. The horses pulling their black, worn, four-seat buggy had become weary from pushing through the swirling snow, and Michael had to whip their flanks again and again to keep them moving. It was not an easy trip for the elderly couple in the buggy either; they were in their mid-fifties and already aching in their bones. The thirty-mile journey from the rural area of St. Martin followed narrow, nearly unmanageable dirt roads with no shoulders and few signs. The buggy swerved and bounced along the icy ruts, and the horses reared and balked repeatedly. But this mission had great significance for Michael and Rosanna, so they pressed on for nearly four hours.

Beyond the Sauk River Bridge and just inside the city limits of St. Cloud, Michael pulled the reins back sharply, and the buggy came to a sudden halt. Just ahead appeared the traditional Great Northern depot sign for St. Cloud, Minnesota. The building behind it was a handsome, newly built granite structure with a steep, dark slate roof. Michael had heard about the new depot in St. Cloud, but he had never had a chance to see it up close. "My God, what a fortress!" he exclaimed to Rosanna. "Must have cost a fortune."

"Hurry, Michael, or we'll be late," Rosanna pleaded. "I think I hear the train coming."

"Now, now, Rosanna, Father Ginther said eleven o'clock. That's fifteen minutes from now," her husband assured her as he helped her down the snow-clogged steps of the buggy and tied the horses to a nearby post. Looking up, he remarked, "By golly, you're right, Rosanna. I can see the headlight through the snow. Come along now. Let's get inside."

The anxious couple made their way through the drifting snow and moved quickly inside the massive granite building where they found a group of Stearns County farm couples milling around, chattering excitedly. Glancing around the room, Michael was awed by the handsome oak-clad pillars and the floor of the depot, but Rosanna didn't notice either. A friend, Sebastian Wimmer, was making his way through the crowd to greet the Murrays, and an important and unusual event was about to happen—the arrival of the Orphan Train.

"I tossed and turned most of the night," Sebastian admitted. "I ordered a girl to take care of the younger children, and now I find that the one coming is only three years old. What will I do about that, Rosanna? I probably should have ordered a boy to help me in the fields in the first place."

"Well, we ordered a girl, too, Sebastian," Rosanna told him, "but that's what we really wanted. With so many of the children married now, it's miserably lonely around our place, and we'll probably need someone to look after us as we get older." Then, as an afterthought, Rosanna added, "This little girl will be useful to me in the kitchen and the garden; in fact, she may well be my salvation some day."

Rosanna Murray was a forceful-looking woman with her piercing blue eyes and graying hair parted in the middle and pulled back sharply into a bun, but there was something about her sallow complexion that hinted at less than robust health. Still her shoulders were held squarely in place, and there was an air of independence about her. She was the kind of level-headed, older woman in whom young girls might confide for direction and advice, but today Rosanna had worry written all over her face.

Rosanna and Michael heard the whistle as the train pulled into the St. Cloud station. With a friendly handshake for their friend, they hurried across the depot to the waiting area. The pot-bellied stove crackled and spit sparks as the stationmaster piled logs on the fire to chase the chill from the room, but the look of the crowd suggested few people concerned themselves with the cold. Only the mysterious Orphan Train occupied their thoughts.

Rosanna's mind raced, and her hands trembled as she and Michael sat down on one of the long oak benches that lined the waiting room. She wondered if she could accept a little girl who was somebody else's child. How would the child fit into her ready-made family? Would her other children think of the girl as a sister or just an intruder?

Touching Michael's arm, Rosanna glanced up at him in hopes of receiving some assurance that they were not making a dreadful mistake. Father Ginther had made it all sound so appealing when he talked about the orphan children from the pulpit. "Why not give it a try," he had suggested. "You would be keeping a homeless child off the streets of New York City, adding another helping hand to the farm crew or perhaps providing yourselves with a nursemaid in your old age." That last suggestion appealed to Rosanna, so she and Michael had signed up for a girl.

Rosanna dug out the indenture papers and number tag from her traveling bag. These had been sent to them by the Sisters of Charity at the New York Foundling Hospital. They would have to sign these papers in front of the Foundling Hospital agent and match their number with the identification worn by their assigned child. This was serious business, and Rosanna's hands continued to tremble as she placed the papers safely back into her bag.

Rosanna had dressed in her Sunday church clothes for the occasion. She wanted the sisters to see that the Murrays were not paupers and, in spite of their age, could provide a good home for an orphan child. She also put on her most assertive air. There must be no mistaking her capabilities.

Weak and shaky as she sometimes felt, she still could put bravado in her step, and she aimed to try today.

The minutes dragged before a tall, thin, grim-faced woman entered the waiting room through the double oak doors of the depot. She wore a long, black, fitted coat with a matching black fedora hat and high-top laced boots. In one hand she carried a sheath of papers, in the other a huge black leather pouch.

"Please stand back, everyone," she began, her shrill voice reaching to everyone in the waiting crowd. "We will be bringing the children in shortly. We want you to be as quiet as possible so as not to frighten them."

An immediate hush fell over the gathering as she spoke. "I am Victoria Grayson, an agent from the New York Foundling Hospital. I have with me forty orphaned children who need places of refuge and some Christian sponsors."

Michael and Rosanna touched hands and smiled at each other.

Miss Grayson continued, "The children have identification tags sewn onto their clothing. Those of you who have requested specific younger children will have them presented to you by a nun from the Sisters of Charity or a nurse who accompanied them on the train. The rest of you may choose from the older children sent by the Foundling Hospital. After you have made your selection, I will be happy to give you any information we might have on your child's background. Please contact me at the agent's desk."

The cold late-October wind whistled through the room as the children entered single file. They appeared to range in age from four to twelve, and they stared straight ahead, some with faces frozen into masks of indifference, others wearing plastic smiles.

Behind the older children and swishing her long black skirt as she walked, a young nun dressed in the religious habit of the Sisters of Charity entered the room. She was smiling openly and clasping the hands of two bewildered little girls, probably two to three years of age. The girls wore long navy coats with flaring caplets and matching bonnets. Each carried a pitifully small cardboard suitcase in her free hand.

The nun's face looked kind and friendly. She chatted with the girls as they walked along. "Come along, children," she bent to whisper. "We're going to find both of you a new mama and papa today."

The nun took her place beside Miss Grayson, keeping her hands tightly clasped around the orphans' little hands. She, too, addressed the group, "My dear friends, I am Sister Felicita. Miss Grayson and I would like to locate the prospective parents of numbers 1152 and 1153. Would holders of these numbers, please come forward."

Realizing that she held number 1153 in her hand, Rosanna Murray nudged her husband, stood up, squared her shoulders and walked forward. Michael followed close behind. Rosanna attempted a smile at Sister Felicita and handed her number 1153. "We are the Murrays," she said. The congenial nun smiled and checked the number carefully.

Sister Felicita spoke to Rosanna. "Mrs. Murray, this is your little girl, Madeline McCarthy. If you will wait with her at one of the benches to the right until I find Rose's new family," she said, gesturing toward the other child she had firmly in hand, "I will join you as soon as possible at the agent's desk."

At first Madeline clung to Sister Felicita and turned her face shyly into the nun's garb. But when Sister Felicita pushed her gently forward, she moved slowly toward Rosanna's out-stretched hand. Michael followed as his wife guided the little girl to one of the long benches where passengers had been waiting for the incoming trains. Then Michael checked the identification tag on the hem of the child's dress and read: Madeline McCarthy, Born New York City, July 22, 1897; Baptized October 5, 1897 (Roman Catholic). #1153.

"That's all there is?" Michael questioned his wife. "Why, she could be some hooligan's child."

"She's pretty enough," observed Rosanna, as she brushed Madeline's long chestnut hair out of her eyes and then picked up the small brown suitcase the child had been clutching.

"Are you sure, Rosanna, t'is what you want? She's so young and so frail looking, and — well, you know, we aren't so young anymore."

"Yes, Michael, she will do just fine," was all Rosanna would say. She drew the little girl to her and assured her-self, "Madeline will be my helper."

Michael walked hesitantly to the agent's desk with the Receipt for Child, which he and Rosanna had signed. Sister

Felicita was flipping through some files of information. "Pardon me, Sister," he began. "I am Michael Murray. My wife and I have accepted Madeline McCarthy. Do you have any further information on her? We would appreciate knowing something more about her."

Sister Felicita flipped quickly to the M's and pulled the information sheet on Madeline McCarthy. "I'm very sorry, Mr. Murray. There is little here on Madeline. It says that she was born in New York City on July 22, 1897, of Irish immigrants John McCarthy and Sarah Dougherty McCarthy, who are listed as deceased." Pointing to the information sheet, she continued, "Madeline was brought to the New York Foundling Hospital at 175 East 68th Street when she was about twelve weeks old. She was baptized by the hospital chaplain Reverend C.M. Thuente, O.P., and was cared for there until last week when she was put on the Orphan Train to the Midwest in response to your request. Her parents named her Madeline Lorraine, and you may keep that name or change it, as you wish."

"That's all you have?" Michael's voice was demanding more.

"Mr. Murray," Sister Felicita continued, gesturing toward the children still in the line-up, "these children are all orphans, street urchins, homeless victims. We bring them here in hopes of finding homes for them on your midwestern farms. Little ones like Madeline were often left in the cribs in our hospital waiting area by destitute parents who could not care for them." Then noting a look of impatience in Michael Murray's eyes, she added, with a spontaneous, reassuring smile, "I think Madeline is a wonderful child, Mr. Murray. She gave us no trouble at all on the long trip from New York."

Sister Felicita spoke briefly to her associate, who was standing with her at the desk, "Please review with Mr. Murray the Receipt for Child, which he and his wife must sign."

Miss Grayson took the Receipt from Michael and read: "We beg to acknowledge receipt of the little orphan as numbered above and promise faithfully to raise said child in the Roman Catholic faith and to send her to school and give her all the advantages that we would give to a child of our own, and report to Sisters of Charity as to health and general condition when requested, notifying them of any change of address."

Miss Grayson looked up at Michael and continued, "If you and your wife are agreeable to these rules, Mr. Murray, you may sign here and take Madeline with you."

Michael Murray tried to steady his hand as he signed the document. He thanked Miss Grayson and Sister Felicita and added, "If it's all right, we'll be going. We want to get the child home before dark."

Leaving the depot, the Murrays passed by Sebastian Wimmer and the little orphan with him. The two orphan girls smiled at each other, unaware of the abiding friendship that would develop between them. Outside, the storm conditions had subsided. A light sprinkling of snow met the Murrays as they left the station with Madeline, her small brown bag again clutched tightly in her hand.

Michael sat in the front seat of the buggy driving the horses while Rosanna rode behind with Madeline. No one spoke on the thirty-mile trip back to St. Martin. Rosanna tried to relax, but images from the past kept rushing through her mind. She could see herself as she had looked arriving in Minnesota many years before with her son Tom, a child from her first marriage to Sean McCaffrey of Lowell, Massachusetts. She had met Michael in St. Martin while visiting her sister, Mary Sullivan. Michael's spouse had also died, leaving him with one daughter, Hannah. Like many Irish immigrants, Michael had come to America to escape the famine and had received a land grant from President Chester A. Arthur for 160 acres of farmland in Stearns County, Minnesota. Rosanna and Michael appreciated each other's situation and married after a short, perfunctory courtship.

They had six children together: two sons, Patrick and Dan, and four daughters, Mary and Margaret, who died prematurely, and then Elizabeth and a second Margaret, both married and raising families of their own. Michael's daughter, Hannah, had become a nun in LaCrosse, Wisconsin. The only one living at the farm was Rosanna's first son, Tom, and she missed her daughters terribly. She knew, too, that she was no longer young and vigorous and had a haunting fear of growing old alone: this, indeed, was why she had so eagerly approached Father Ginther about the Orphan Train.

Madeline stirred, and Rosanna spoke to her, "Are you all right, child?"

Madeline did not respond. Exhausted by a day of fear and uncertainty, she had fallen asleep, and her treasured bag of belongings had fallen slowly to the floor of the buggy.

Only by late afternoon did the travelers approach the Murray farm. The encircling birches, poplars, and maples stood barren, and the cornfields, cut close the ground, wore a thin coat of newly fallen snow. Madeline was awakened by the raspy voice of a man riding horseback beside the buggy, "I see you got yourself a wee one, Rosanna. Good luck to you!" he shouted as he rode on ahead.

"That's your new neighbor, John Flynn, Madeline," Rosanna said. "He's a smart one. Don't mind his blather."

The child remained quiet, overwhelmed by the strange sights and sounds around her. The bustling New York Foundling Hospital and the familiar faces of Sister Felicita and her little friends had already faded in her memory.

The Murray farm presented a sharp contrast to the rows of brownstone buildings crowded into the streets of New York City. A huge red barn to the left of the farmhouse and several smaller red buildings made up the complex. The house itself, a white, two-story, clapboard structure, had an open porch in the front. A dim light shone from the window as the buggy stopped at the front steps.

"We're here, young lady." Michael spoke to the sleepy child for the first time since leaving the depot. Then he picked her up with his strong farmer's hands and lifted her down from the buggy. "Come with us, Madeline."

The tiny waif followed Rosanna up the steps onto the porch, and there the two waited for Michael to tie up the horses. No one met them at the door, but at least it was warm inside. There was a steep, narrow stairway opposite the front door and a hallway to the right. As Madeline shuffled along the hallway, she saw only the long, dark pieces of scruffy wood on which she was walking and the backs of Michael's boots. She was entering a different world from any she had known before.

A tall, young man in heavy, gray pants, much like the ones Michael wore, greeted them as they entered the parlor. "This is your big brother, Madeline," Rosanna explained. "Tom, this is Madeline."

Tom McCaffrey nodded to the child and then turned to his mother. "She's so little, Ma, and so fragile looking. Shouldn't you have picked an older child?"

"She'll do just fine, Tom. Now I think we all need a good meal," she added, as she proceeded into the kitchen and bent to gather wood for the stove.

During the evening meal of Irish stew and corn bread, no one mentioned the journey. Tom questioned his stepfather about renting out some of their 160 acres of land to the Flynns next door. He was adamant about reducing the workload. Trying to convince Michael, he emphasized, "You aren't getting any younger, Pa, and John Flynn needs another fifty acres for corn."

Michael Murray frowned. "We can manage, Tom, and don't be mindin' my business for me. When it's time to quit, I'll quit. Now that's enough." Knowing when to bow out,

Tom McCaffrey stood up and walked across the kitchen to the wood range for a cup of tea.

The Murray kitchen was the largest room in the house. It had two long, narrow windows on the outer wall and was painted a dour mustard yellow. Beside the huge wood range stood a rectangular wood box stacked with freshly cut birch logs and random pieces of kindling. A long trestle table occupied the middle of the kitchen with space for at least ten, and the oak benches that accompanied it showed signs of wear. White pine cupboards with black wrought-iron handles lined the kitchen walls. They, too, carried the scars of many years' use. Attached to the wall beside the back door, a strip of black wire hooks provided a place for the jackets, caps, and other outer wear worn in the farm fields. Especially strange to Madeline as she shyly glanced around the room was the tall wooden box next to the sink where Tom had gone to get milk for his tea. It looked like something she had once seen in the kitchen of the Foundling Hospital.

Madeline sat at the table next to Rosanna, and the two men sat side-by-side across from them, elbows spread wide, eager to attack the stew. To the small child, the men looked like giants, but actually Michael Murray was a very short, slight man. He had deep hazel eyes, dark shaggy eyebrows and an unkempt, graying moustache. Thirty years of tilling the soil, milking cows and working long hours in the summer sun, had masked his face with deep grooves and wrinkles, especially around his eyes. Tom, tall and broad shouldered, had blue eyes and sandy hair, like his mother. As the two men devoured the savory stew, Rosanna turned to Madeline. "Are you hungry, child?"

Madeline nodded. The Irish stew felt warm and friendly inside her, and the corn bread melted quickly in her mouth.

Chapter Two
The Farmer's Daughter

MORNING CAME EARLY ON THE MURRAY FARM. On a December morning at 5:00 A.M., six-year-old Madeline could hear Papa and Tom stumbling down the narrow stairway from the second floor, under the influence of the whiskey they had drunk the night before.

"God damn, I'm freezin' to death," Papa complained in his usual morning greeting to Rosanna. "Is there a drop of tea in the house? And the mush . . . I hope you made extra 'cause I'll be needin' it today to keep my bones together. Must be twenty degrees in here."

Rosanna ignored Michael's grumpy talk in the morning and poured him an extra-large cup of extra-strong tea. That settled him down until she could dish up the oatmeal, scrambled eggs, and sausage. Then she flipped several slices of her homemade bread on the oven rack and produced some slightly burned toast, which she served with her homemade raspberry jam. The toast and jam was Tom's favorite part of the meal. He sat beside Papa but never said a word until Papa had finished his breakfast.

Madeline could hear their conversation through the grated openings in her bedroom floor. Yawning freely, she sat up, flipped her quilt down and watched the collected bits of frost fly though the air. Then she took a deep breath and followed the white vapor trail as it floated lazily toward the ceiling. With a small wool blanket, which she still took to bed with her each night, she wrapped herself snugly and pulled up her bed socks. Then for several minutes she sat on the edge of her bed like a miniature mummy and waited for the right time to go downstairs for breakfast. That, of course, would be after Papa had quieted down. For a brief moment Madeline's eyes searched the empty walls of her room until they rested on the crooked cross above her bed. "Help me today, sweet Jesus," she whispered. "Help Mama and Papa to love me."

Madeline's room resembled a monk's cell, except that it was probably more austere. The antique crucifix with the corpus ajar, to which she had just spoken, hung at a slight angle over her bed. Madeline had decided long ago that it hung there to protect her from ghosts, mice, and the anger of Papa on a bad day. Next to the only window in the room stood a four-drawer maple commode, which held all of her personal possessions. The top drawer contained her hip-high black stockings, her bloomers, and two woolen scarves, a red one that Rosanna had knit for her when she was four and a navy blue one that John Flynn's wife had given her for her sixth birthday. In drawer two, Madeline stored the little brown bag she had carried with her on the Orphan Train. Rosanna had told her she could keep it as long as she didn't take it out of her bedroom; Madeline was to live in the present not the past. Beside the brown bag, the little girl stored a small bag of hard sugar candies that Papa had brought her from the general store in St. Martin on a good day when he was paid a generous price for a sick hog. Drawer three held her petticoats and two pairs of leggings, which were at least two to three inches too long for her. In the bottom drawer, she kept her shoes and boots. Her three dresses hung from hooks on the back of the door.

She had no closet in the pitifully small room, only a recessed niche for her milk glass chamber pot, which Madeline thought was the prettiest thing in the room. She had cried when she chipped the scalloped lid on the day after her fifth birthday as she hurriedly carried it down the long, wooden stairway to the outhouse.

Before venturing down the creaky steps, Madeline waited to hear the kitchen door slam, which meant that Papa and Tom had gone out to the barn. Then she carried her day's clothes in a neat little bundle down the steps to the kitchen where she could dress behind the crackling fire of the wood stove and warm her bloomers before she put them on. As she dawdled behind the stove, enjoying the warmth of the fire, Rosanna called to her, "Come out, lazy-bones, and eat. The mush is getting cold, and first thing you know I'll be havin' to gather the eggs myself. T'is baking day, you know." Rosanna's sleepless night with a jar of

The Murrays in 1904 or 1907. Dan and Michael with Rosanna and Madeline in front.

hot water at her feet and mittens on her hands sometimes left her blurry-eyed and cranky.

Gathering the eggs was only one of the tasks the frail six-year-old did each morning. She enjoyed the job, except in the winter. The chicken coop stayed warm most of the year from all the chickens huddled together, but in the winter it was miserably cold both outside and inside the coop, and it was miserably dark—especially at 6:00 A.M. As she gathered the delicate white treasures, Madeline repeated to herself, "Careful, careful, girl. Mama's broom stings when you are clumsy."

Madeline learned quickly how to become a farmer's daughter. By age seven she had learned how to squeeze the cow's teats firmly but gently in her hand to fill her pail with breakfast milk. She talked to Bessie as she watched the milk stream into her pail. "Good morning, Bessie. Are you happy to see me? I like to visit you because I'm lonely. Mama is getting sicker every day, and some days I think Papa hates me." Then she quietly sang her Holstein friend a tune, "When Irish Eyes Are Smiling," which John Flynn had taught her one day when he was waiting for Papa to come in from the fields. "How I wish Mama and Papa's Irish eyes would smile more often, Bessie."

At age seven, Madeline was sent to a one-room country school located between the Murray farm and St. Martin. She loved the big iron bell in the belfry tower and made a valiant effort to get to school on time just to hear it ring at nine o'clock. Mr. Lutgen, the schoolmaster, soon recognized Madeline's intelligence and encouraged her to read and practice her numbers, both at school and at home. Since she had to walk two miles to school in good weather and bad, Madeline seldom went to school in the winter. As long as the weather remained mild, she enjoyed the walk with Agnes and Dorothy, her two country neighbors, but in January and February when fierce winds drifted snow across the narrow rural roads, she seldom risked the danger of frostbite or of being marooned far from home.

After one bitterly cold walk to school in mid-December, Madeline approached her teacher with something she had been yearning to ask for weeks. "Mr. Lutgen, would you have an extra book that I could keep at home in the winter? I love reading. It's my favorite subject, but my toes are almost frozen this morning, and my mother isn't well."

Mr. Lutgen placed a comforting hand on her shoulder. "Of course, Madeline, I don't know how you manage to get here as often as you do when it's so blustery outside. I'll fill your schoolbag with as many books as possible when you leave today. No need to return them until spring. Books are good for the soul, Madeline. Make friends with them and you'll never be lonely."

"Oh, thank you, Mr. Lutgen. Did you know that I want to be a teacher just like you when I grow up," she replied, with a grateful smile. Mr. Lutgen smiled, too.

When Madeline had completed the fifth grade, the Murrays decided that they had complied with the rules of indenture and needed her to help at home. The books Mr. Lutgen gave her to keep became her dearest treasure, and she frequently read late into the night until she knew each book by heart.

Madeline often walked to church in St. Martin on Sundays. When Rosanna was no longer able to go to church, especially in the wintertime, Michael did not attend either. But Madeline was expected to go, even if she had to walk. Sometimes the Flynns or some other kind neighbor picked her up along the way; other times she made the trip alone. The pastor would greet her at the door, "Good morning, Madeline. How are your mother and father today?" Madeline wished that he would ask how she was doing, but he seldom did. Every Sunday while Father Eisenhof offered his Mass in Latin and gave his long, fist-banging sermon in German, Madeline prayed for deliverance. On the way home she

Madeline's Solemn Communion, about age thirteen.

often stamped her feet defiantly and raised her fists to heaven in frustration, for the little Irish girl had not understood a word that had been spoken in the service.

Piano lessons brought frustration, too. On Saturdays Madeline walked to St. Martin for lessons, which Rosanna wanted her to take "so someone would use the piano in the parlor." She actually loved playing the piano, but she hated when Miss Christen would thump her fingers with a thimble if she played a wrong note or came a few minutes late. One day as she approached the outskirts of town, she found a seemingly endless freight train straddling the tracks and blocking her path to Miss Christen's house. "If I stand here waiting any longer," Madeline spoke thoughtfully to herself, "Miss Christen will rap my knuckles worse than last week, and Mama will be angry, too. Maybe if I hurry, I can cross between the cars before they start again." And with that, she hoisted herself onto the tongue connecting the freight cars and leaped triumphantly to the other side. As she picked herself up, she heard the sound of the train chugging forward, and her heart began to pound uncontrollably. That adventure Madeline tucked deep into her memory box and threw away the key.

Except for her piano playing, there was little entertainment in Madeline's young life; however, a spring or summer rainstorm delighted her. When the thunder rolled and jagged streaks of lightning lit up the sky, Madeline climbed up on her bed and listened to the rain pounding on the roof overhead, or she pressed her face against her windowpane and watched the wind whip straw and chicken feathers across the farmyard. Sometimes she saw Papa and Tom running from the barn to the shed with their kerosene lanterns swaying, trying to secure the doors and clear the downspouts. This brought a shiver of excitement to the little girl's body, and she came to love storms rather than fear them.

At age twelve, she was already in the fields pitching bundles of hay on to tall, makeshift hayracks. Jabbing and heaving with the rugged pitchforks produced marble-sized blisters on her fingers, and the oppressive summer sun beat mercilessly on her aching young back. On observing this, her friend John Flynn approached Michael and told him he was working the young girl much too hard. After that Madeline worked mainly with Rosanna in the house or in the farmyard garden.

Kitchen chores were more to Madeline's liking. She loved to help Rosanna make lunches for the threshers and then deliver them to the workers in the fields with her wooden wagon. All the threshers came to know Madeline and waved and whistled as she approached. "Good morning, lass," they would call. "You're lookin' mighty pretty today." This turned Madeline's cheeks scarlet, and she hurried off to serve another crew of threshers, secretly delighting in the small attention paid to her.

As Michael and Rosanna grew older and more infirm, they became more dependent on Madeline. In 1913, when she was sixteen, they purchased a Model T Ford from a farm-to-farm salesman with the idea that she could drive them to town for shopping and to weddings and funerals. Henry Ford's affordable new "Tin Lizzy" was making the horse and buggy obsolete, and Madeline became the designated driver of the horseless carriage as soon as it was delivered.

"Get in, young lady, and I'll show you how this marvelous machine works," suggested the salesman.

Madeline was dumbfounded by the suggestion, amazed that Papa would let her drive this marvelous machine by herself? "Oh! I . . . I couldn't," she sputtered.

Papa interrupted with an unexpected vote of confidence. "Of course, you can, Madeline. You're twice as smart as I am. Now get in."

For thirty minutes the Ford salesman escorted the frightened adolescent down the dusty, rural roads leading from the Murray farm. His instructions were very specific.

"First you have your papa crank the engine the way I just did, Madeline. When the little beauty is purring nicely, you put your left foot on the clutch pedal, like this. Now you have to shift into first gear, like this. You follow me?"

Madeline nodded and watched intently. "When you let the clutch pedal out, you step on the gas pedal, ever so gently, like this. Don't press too hard or you will jerk ahead and the motor will die."

Madeline's heart raced, and her face felt hot and sweaty as she listened to the detailed instructions: "Just remember, Madeline, that the four gears in the car form an "H." First gear is down on the left side of the "H." Then back to the center bar—like this; then up to the high right for second gear—like this; then straight down on the right side of the "H" for third. Reverse is up the left side. Use your clutch in the same way for each gear. You follow me?"

"When you want to stop, you put your left foot on the clutch and you take your right foot off the gas pedal and put it on the brake—like this." The car came to an abrupt stop, shooting clouds of dust into the air behind the rear wheels. "Now you try it," urged the salesman.

Madeline exchanged seats with the salesman. Her first try was disastrous. The Ford sputtered, choked and died. Succeeding attempts got progressively better and finally led to a miraculous trip down the country road toward St. Martin and back to the farm.

"You've got it!" cheered the impatient salesman. "And now I must be getting back to town." With that he prepared to leave with the partner who had accompanied him to the Murray farm. He gave Michael a title card and a contract to sign and then hastily tucked Michael's five hundred dollars into his brown calf wallet. "Enjoy the car," he called back, as he disappeared down the road, leaving a bewildered sixteen-year old with only her own ingenuity and a new Model T Ford.

That night as she lay in her upstairs bedroom listening through the floor grates to Papa telling Rosanna about the car deal, Madeline turned to the leaning figure on the cross and sighed, "Now it's all up to You."

Chapter Three
Looking to the Future

LIFE ON THE MURRAY FARM WAS a mixed blessing for Madeline. She was there for a specific purpose, and she knew it. The calluses on her hands and the often sad and empty look in her eyes told her story. Her room on the second floor of the old farmhouse did little to provide a refuge from the harsh winter weather, and frequent outbursts from her aging foster parents devastated her spirit. But there were redeeming moments.

Rosanna gave Madeline many coveted tips on cooking and baking during her teen years, as the two worked side by side in the big farm kitchen. Pies were high on Rosanna's priority list, and her instructions were clear. "Remember always to use cold water for your pie crust, Madeline. It makes the shell flaky. With a fork, you must cut the lard into different sized pieces. Place the pie, especially if it is a fruit pie, on the bottom shelf of the oven; otherwise, your crust will be soggy." Fearful of her mother's anger and eager to please her, the young apprentice made mental notes of all of these instructions, and eventually she turned out pies that rivaled her mother's.

With bread making, too, Rosanna had special rules: "The dough must rise in a safe, dark place away from drafts and loud noises. Let it rise, Madeline, until it is twice its size; too little will make the dough tough, and too much will cause holes in the slices." Rosanna's culinary skills were well known and respected in the neighborhood, and Madeline never forgot those rules.

Rosanna excelled in other domestic skills, too, particularly crocheting. Every corner of the Murray home displayed her handiwork—doilies, blankets, tablecloths, shawls, mittens, and scarves. The woman's health was failing, but her fingers remained nimble and talented. Those talented fingers remained beautiful as well. Long and slender with nails that Rosanna meticulously clipped and then rounded with a pumice stone, they were the fingers of an artist. The artist then advised her daughter, "It makes a house a home, Madeline, to have your own creations around the place; and, glory be to God, we can't afford to buy flourishes. So we must try, girl, to spruce up the place on our own." Under her mother's supervision, Madeline learned the arts of knitting and crocheting and turned out beautiful cross-stitch pillowcases, too. When she felt up to it, Rosanna enjoyed working with her protege, and the blossoming young woman appreciated her ailing mother's efforts.

Madeline continued in her domestic role on the Murray farm until some time in 1915, when some of the young people in the St. Martin area began leaving home to join the army or to find jobs in the bigger cities. She longed to leave the farm, too. More than anything, she wanted an education. Any kind of education would help, but she especially loved books and still dreamed of being a teacher.

After one Sunday Mass, Madeline had a long talk with her friend, Rose, who had come on the Orphan Train with her and was now living with the Thelen family in St. Martin. Rose and Madeline often met after church to talk about the week's happenings and what, if anything, they were planning to do in the days ahead. "I'm leaving in the fall, Madeline," Rose told her that Sunday. "I'm going to go to business school in St. Cloud." Rose's eyes glowed with anticipation of this adventure. "My family wants me to learn a skill, so I can get a job. Why don't you come with me?"

"Oh, Rose, you're so lucky," said Madeline with regret. "If only I could go. I'm eighteen now, you know, so I could leave, but Mama's health is failing. Sometimes she has a hard time breathing, and with Tom gone, I'm all she has. I couldn't leave her." Madeline was close to tears, but she forced a smile. "Please write to me, Rose. I'll look forward to your letters. Tell me all about school and about the young men you meet in the city." Then tears streamed down Madeline's cheeks.

Rose took her friend's hand and squeezed it. "I will! I will! I wish you could come with me, Madeline. I hate to leave you." The two girls hugged each other as if their hearts were breaking. They had been friends for most their lives.

After Rose left, Madeline found the farm work harder to bear. She fed the pigs and chickens, helped Michael milk the cows, weeded and harvested the garden for Rosanna, baked bread and even learned to sew. Once a month she took Michael and Rosanna to Albany in the Model T to shop for supplies. Occasionally, she even went to a dance with her friend Johnny Lauer. And she dreamed about meeting a young man the Murrays would like so that she could have a home and family of her own.

In 1918, with the war in Europe over, the Murrays' son Dan came home from North Dakota, where he had been employed on a government construction crew. With Tom married and living in St. Cloud, Michael Murray discussed with Dan the possibility of selling the farm. At seventy-one, he couldn't do the heavy work alone. "Maybe it's time to sell the farm, Dan," he confided. "Mama is sick, and I'm not getting any younger. T'would be givin' up my life's work, but . . ."

"Now, Pa, don't talk like that," Dan interrupted. "I'll stay on and help you out. I'm thinkin' Mama would like that, too. She's lookin' so pale and weak. I was shocked when I first saw her this time. There's no spring in her step anymore."

"I won't be havin' ya stay out of duty, son," Michael continued, ignoring the reference to Rosanna. "But if ya really want to give the land a chance again, I'd be happy to have ya join me."

Dan read the message well and stayed on, and he and Madeline made the place productive again.

On sleepless nights, Madeline often lay in her bed upstairs in the farmhouse luxuriating in her own private thoughts, appreciating even this tiny place of privacy, thinking about her past and her future. She wondered, of course, what path her life would have taken if her natural parents had not abandoned her so many years ago, or, perhaps what her life would have been like had she been taken in by a more appreciative, loving family in New York. Perhaps she would be a teacher now or a nurse. She wondered also when she would ever get away from the farm, which for her had no appeal at all. And, of course, she wondered if she would ever have a husband and family of her own. Her mind held a plethora of questions, but there were no answers.

Almost four years later, Madeline finally had the courage to talk with Rosanna about going to school in St. Cloud. Taking her mother to the front porch, she pleaded in private, "Mama, I want so much to go to school again. I'm twenty-five, and I want to go to business school like Rose did. She has a good job in the bank in Albany now. Would you talk to Tom about this, Mama . . . please?"

Rosanna listened and finally agreed. Tom McCaffrey, who had married into a family associated with the business school in St. Cloud, came home to visit one weekend and agreed to help. The following nine months in St. Cloud answered many of Madeline's questions.

Chapter Four
The Blossoming

ON THE FIRST DAY OF SCHOOL at the St. Cloud Business School, Madeline took her place at a long, oak table occupied by seven other students. Small nicks and scratches and the initials "R.D." scarred the surface of the table, and the stools stood so high that Madeline's feet barely reached the support wrung. But these incidentals did nothing to diminish the eager young woman's delight at being in school again.

Madeline had just taken out her notepad and pencil to record the teacher's instructions when she noticed a dark, handsome young man enter the side door of the classroom. He stood about five feet, ten inches tall and was clean-shaven. His jet-black hair was slicked back from his forehead, and he had enormous brown eyes. The young man wore neat-looking tan trousers and a brown bulky-knit sweater. Madeline's heart skipped at least one beat. She was used to men with heavy moustaches, beards, and ill-fitting farm clothes. The young man took a seat at the table ahead of her and also took out a notepad and a fountain pen. As Mr. Beardsley, the teacher, went around the room asking for the students' names, the handsome young man identified himself as William Matthews from the Foley area. Madeline jotted that name on her notepad. After the introductions, Mr. Beardsley began his welcoming words to the class. He concluded by saying, "Our goal is to see that all of you find purposeful employment after taking this class." That comment found a home in Madeline's heart.

Two days later, in the downstairs lunchroom of the school, Madeline and William encountered each other for the first time. Madeline was sitting at a small table near a window in the back of the room, surveying the street outside. She saw a uniformed policeman walking past the school on his morning beat and noticed a shaggy Irish Setter relieving himself on a telephone pole as a young couple walked arm-in-arm down the street. My, how different the scene was from the view outside her bedroom window at the farm.

"Mind if I sit down?"

Madeline turned to see William Matthews smiling down at her. In a shy, boyish manner, he waited for a reply.

Madeline's face turned crimson, and her voice faltered, "Why yes . . . well, of course, please sit down."

"I'm new here and I don't know a soul. I thought it would be nice to eat with someone," William began. "I believe your name is Madeline. I'm in your Employment

Preparation class, and I remember that name." William was even better looking close up. His thick black eyebrows framed his eyes in an intriguing way, and those big brown eyes had a soft, soulful look.

Madeline could feel a flush in her cheeks and a flutter in her stomach. "I'm just having a sandwich, William, but you certainly can sit with me," she replied.

"Just call me Will. Most of my friends do," said the eager young man, as he pulled out a chair, making that screeching sound that assaults the ears.

Madeline picked nervously at her sandwich, conscious that Will was watching her. Will took note of her petite figure, which probably weighed no more than a hundred pounds. Her eyes were bright green, clear and sparkling; and the small, round, rimless eyeglasses that covered them balanced precariously down a bit from the bridge of her nose. The girl's skin was as clear and creamy as a cloistered nun's, no powder or rouge, and her long chestnut hair fell from a band at her neckline into generous waves around her shoulders. *She's a thoroughbred all right*, Will thought, as he continued his efforts to make conversation with the pretty young woman.

"Do you like to dance, Madeline?" he asked, hoping they might have something in common.

The unusual question took Madeline by surprise. "Well, I do dance, Will. I'm not the world's greatest, but I've been to the New Munich Ballroom a few times."

Will felt encouraged. "I love to dance, and it's the best exercise I know. There's a ballroom in Foley, too, and I go there every chance I get." Happy with the progress he had made, Will continued, "Do you think I could walk you home from school, Madeline? Maybe we could get to know each other." Then glancing at the clock on the lunchroom wall, he added, "Maybe we'd better get back to class now. It's almost one o'clock." They parted company then, promising to meet after class at the front door of the school.

Madeline couldn't get Will out of her thoughts during her Office Procedures class. She vaguely remembered hearing the teacher talk about how to answer an office phone properly and how to file important documents, but she was really more concerned about how to explain the presence of Will Matthews to her foster brother Tom and his wife after school. She wondered, too, if they would tell Michael and Rosanna about her new friend.

To Madeline's great relief, Tom and Jean McCaffrey were not at home when the young couple arrived about four o'clock. Grateful for the favor but anxious, Madeline bid Will a hasty goodbye at the front door, but only after she had agreed to take a walk around Lake George with him after lunch the following day. In parting, Will made the suggestion, "If you bring a sandwich again tomorrow, maybe we could eat lunch together in the park."

That evening when the last of the supper dishes had been safely returned to their cupboards, Madeline excused herself and retreated to the McCaffrey's backyard. There she glided back and forth in the garden swing, breathing in the intoxicating scents of the fall season. Nature had painted a thrilling picture featuring red sugar maples, deeper magenta pin oaks, and the faded remnants of a rock garden once filled with multi-colored petunias, marigolds, and snapdragons. Yes, there was life beyond the Murray farm. Yes! Yes! freedom, challenges, and the promise of tomorrow.

Lake George was only a short distance from the business school, and it provided some interesting conversation as the two students strolled along its banks the next day. Madeline told Will about the dangers of the small, wily lake, dangers that Tom had warned her about just a few nights earlier. "Don't step off the path, Will," she cautioned. "There's treacherous quicksand along the shore. Years ago, they say, two little children were sucked down by the ugly, slimy mud."

Will laughed at the grim story and assured Madeline that it was probably just an old wives' tale, but he followed single file behind her and did not step beyond the path.

The two friends rejoiced in their common background. They were strangers in the city, both seeking a better life, perhaps some new friends and, above all, an education. Both of them turned out to be orphans of sorts, too. Though born in Midland, Michigan, Will had lived with his aunt, Nora Connally, on a farm near Foley since he was nine months old. His mother had died after his birth, and his father had decided he could not raise the boy alone. Madeline attempted to explain her humble beginnings, her arrival on the Orphan Train, and life on the Murray farm, too, but her references to the Murrays were intentionally vague. No need to hurry the introductions of Michael and Rosanna. That might come at considerable risk.

The nine months at the business school passed all too quickly for Madeline. Occasionally, she went with Will to the New Munich Ballroom in Nora Connally's Model T. Will dressed neatly in a long-sleeved, blue shirt and tweed trousers and wore leather-soled shoes that glided smoothly over the dance floor. Madeline, in her mid-calf dress and ankle-high boots, tried hard to follow him as he twirled her around the pavilion, but he was unquestionably the better dancer of the two. "Just relax a little, Madeline," Will suggested, "and feel the rhythm of the music." But being held close in the young man's arms exhilarated Madeline so much that she simply held on tight and hoped for the best. After the dancing, they enjoyed a glass of beer together and talked about school.

Sometimes after classes the two students repeated their walk around Lake George. Their walk often ended with a visit to Holy Angels Church. Holy Angels was a few blocks from the lake and was the place where the McCaffreys had been attending Mass since the Church of the Immaculate Conception on St. Germain had burned to the ground in August of 1920. During one visit, a defining moment arrived.

As Will followed Madeline down the side aisle of the church, she suddenly stopped, genuflected, signed herself and entered a pew next to the Fourth Station of the Cross, Jesus Meets His Mother. Will followed her into the pew where the two knelt and attempted to pray. Barely into her second Hail Mary, Madeline felt Will nudge her gently. "Madeline," he whispered, "I think I love you, and I want to marry you."

If they had not been in church, Madeline would have shouted for joy, but, as things were, she looked up at Will, her heart beating wildly, and whispered back, "I love you, too, Will." From then on, the two were inseparable.

Now committed to each other, Madeline and Will picked a balmy Sunday in mid-April to drive to St. Martin and the Murray farm. They chose the route west on Highway 52 through the village of Waite Park with its large Great Northern Carshops, past St. John's Abbey and Avon, on the shores of lovely Spunk Lake, to Albany, the village where Madeline had often taken Michael and Rosanna to shop for supplies. Will enjoyed the travelogue that Madeline provided as they motored through the countryside.

"I'm amazed that the towns are so close together. Seems to be a waste of good farm land," Will commented, as they approached Albany.

"Oh, there's a good reason for that," Madeline explained. "Five to seven miles was considered a good day's ride on a horse in days gone by. People didn't always have Tin Lizzies like this, you know."

"You're absolutely right, smartie. Why didn't I think of that?"

At Albany, Madeline instructed Will to follow Route 10. This rough gravel road led south to St. Martin.

"Looks like good soil," Will observed, as they passed acres of rolling farmland.

"With good weather, it produces a generous amount of hay, corn, and oats," Madeline replied. "At least that's what the Murrays always planted."

Then Will changed the subject completely. "I hope your parents will like me. I'm getting a little nervous."

"They'd better," Madeline said definitively. Then both of them caught sight of the Murray's mailbox sign at the side of the road.

Rosanna met them at the door, weak and pale, with a calico cat in one hand and a walking stick in the other. "And who do we have here, Madeline?" she asked in surprise, seeing the handsome young man close at Madeline's side.

Madeline's and Will's Wedding Photo.
June 17, 1924

"This is Will, Mama. I wanted you and Papa to meet him. May we come in?"

Rosanna led them to the kitchen where she poured them a cup of hot tea and then limped slowly to the back doorway to call Michael from the barn. "Come, Michael, Madeline is here — with a friend."

Slowly Michael limped his way to the house, muttering inaudible profanities. After brief introductions, he suddenly offered Will a shot of Irish whiskey, which the young man reluctantly accepted.

"Thank you, Mr. Murray," Will said. "It's certainly a pleasure to meet you, sir."

The old man ignored the pleasantries and got down to business, for he could easily see that the young couple had a definite agenda. "Is it our blessin' you're wantin', Madeline?" he questioned, in his usual gruff manner. "We sent ya to school to learn somethin', not to be gadding about with the menfolk."

Embarrassed and humiliated, Madeline turned to Rosanna for help. "Mama," she said, her eyes glassy with tears, "Will and I want to get married, and I wanted you and Papa to meet Will and see what a fine man he is."

Rosanna had pity on the struggling couple and invited them for supper. "It's only the usual we'll be having, Will, but you are welcome to stay. It's a long way back to St. Cloud."

Michael took Will out to the barn then to show him his Holsteins, while Rosanna and Madeline prepared the evening meal. Madeline noticed how unsteady Rosanna had become as the two stood at the kitchen sink peeling potatoes. "Mama, are you feeling all right?" she asked, but Rosanna chose to ignore the question.

After supper, fearful of more outbursts from Michael, Madeline and Will excused themselves and hurried back to the security of the city.

Barely into their return journey, Will turned to Madeline. "I don't think your father likes me," he said. "He seemed upset all the while we were there."

"That's his nature, Will," Madeline explained. "I've had to live with his grumpiness all my life. He's had a hard life on the farm and before that, too. I try to overlook his ways because he's very good to Mama." And then she added, "I don't know what he would do without her."

They needed two more trips to St. Martin to arrange their wedding at the church. On June 17, 1924, the exuberant bride and her nervous but excited groom were married with the Murrays' blessings — or at least Rosanna's. The bride wore an ankle-length white dress trimmed with lace, which she had sewn herself, and on her head a veil with a band of seed pearls and white carnations. Will looked handsome in a black vested suit with white tuxedo shirt and white bow tie. The entire Murray family attended, as well as Madeline's friend Rose, who was now married and living in Waite Park. Nora Connally also attended, but no one else from Will's family. Father Eugene Woerdehoff, O.S.B., celebrated the Mass, and the attendants were Leo Casey, Will's cousin, and Loretta Murray, Madeline's niece. All of the Irish families from the St. Martin area came to celebrate, including the Flynns, the Shays, and the Sinclairs; and many German families came as well. That evening brandy and Irish whiskey flowed freely at the Murray farm.

Chapter Five
A Nightmare of Nurturing

ROSANNA MURRAY'S HEART HAD BEEN failing for many years. No doubt she had known as much when, at fifty-two, she had sent for the little orphan girl. Life on a midwestern farm had not been easy for her, and now that Madeline was married, her support system had virtually vanished. Rosanna had been the starter for the whole Murray family, as well as a confidant for the neighborhood women, and a well-respected member of the St. Martin farming community. When she died in April of 1927, the quality of life on the Murray farm deteriorated dramatically. "Nothing seems worthwhile anymore," Michael complained to his son Dan one evening on the farmhouse porch. In St. Cloud, Madeline felt strangely lost, too. Rosanna had been the only mother she had ever known. And although Rosanna had sometimes been harsh and demanding, Madeline wanted to remember only the kind and helpful things that her mother had done for her.

Madeline was now a mother herself. Her first baby, a boy, was named LeRoy after Will's favorite cousin, LeRoy Couchman. LeRoy had jet-black hair like Will's and lively green eyes like Madeline's, but as he grew, he looked more and more like his mother. Barely eighteen months later, a second baby arrived, named RoseAnn after Madeline's mother. RoseAnn looked like Will, with black hair and slate-colored eyes that soon turned brown. The two children delighted Madeline and Will, who now had what they had always wanted, a family of their own.

Happy as the grateful parents were, they still had grave concerns about Papa Murray and Dan. Madeline knew in her heart that the two would not survive long on the Murray farm. "Perhaps we should have Papa and Dan stay with us for a while, Will," Madeline suggested one evening, slowly weighing the thought as she spoke. "It wouldn't be easy with the children under foot, but I think we could manage for a while." Madeline's sense of obligation outweighed her common sense, and she knew it. The idea, however, was put on hold for over a year when Madeline discovered she was pregnant with a third child. Mary was born in late November.

Finally, in the fall of 1929, just when the Great Depression loomed, Michael and Dan and the Model T Ford came to live with Madeline and Will and their three small children at 120 Seventeenth Avenue South in St. Cloud. The house, a modest, two-story, white frame house had a porch in front, a small garage located next to the alley, and a large garden plot in between. The back entry of the house opened into the kitchen, which contained a drop-leaf breakfast table with four chairs, a four-burner gas stove, a wooden icebox, and a large free-standing cupboard with a cast-iron sink in the middle of the counter. The adjacent dining room and parlor were separated by an archway, and opposite the front door, a steep wooden stairway led to a bathroom at the head of the stairs and three bedrooms. Madeline and Will shared one bedroom with Baby Mary. LeRoy and RoseAnn shared the second bedroom, and Grandpa and Dan the third. There was no privacy for anyone, and Grandpa and Dan did little to promote cooperation and peace.

"God damn it, Madeline, where did you hide my bottle?" often prefaced Michael's frequent tirades, and the two men's filthy habit of spitting carelessly at a spittoon upset the whole family. But the greatest worry to Madeline and Will was the constant flow of pipe smoke curling through the house. Madeline pleaded with Dan, hoping he would deliver her message to Michael. "Please, Dan, don't blow pipe smoke into the children's faces. They're so little, and their lungs are very tender."

The culprits ignored her pleading, however, and Will felt helpless to intervene. This posed a difficult situation for him; he felt grateful to Michael for some limited financial help, but he was completely disgusted by the older man's behavior, especially toward the children, who were now four, two-and-a-half and seven months of age.

Dan soon found a job on a construction crew at the Garfield School, which was being built directly across the street from the Matthews' home. To Madeline's relief, Dan worked days and caroused nightly at the local bars with his crew. But Grandpa lingered around the house most of the time, causing Madeline one problem after another.

Grandpa missed the farm terribly, and he grew more depressed and senile as the months passed. On several occasions, he ran away to the Murray farm, which was now rented by a neighboring farmer, Ed Sinclair. His usual pattern was to flag down the Greyhound bus driver on Highway 52 and beg for a ride to Albany. Feeling sorry for an old man standing beside the highway, hitchhiking in only his shirtsleeves, the driver would pick him up and drop him off again with other Albany-bound passengers, hoping he would find his way from there.

"Damn grateful to you, lad," Grandpa always said to the driver, as he stumbled off the bus and started his trek to the Murray farm. Sometimes an old friend or even a stranger picked up the old man and took him down Route 10 toward St. Martin. "Much obliged," Michael would say with a mischievous grin. "No place like home."

When Ed Sinclair returned to the farmhouse from his work in the fields, he would find Michael Murray sitting on the front porch waiting to attack him verbally and physically. "Damn you, Sinclair! Get off my land. You son-of-a-bitch, you're robbin' me blind." Then Ed would have to arrange to take Michael back to St. Cloud. These outrageous maneuvers embarrassed Madeline and Will, but more was to come.

On a hot July afternoon, Madeline heard a knock on the Matthews' back door. The neighborhood grocer, Cliff

Beaulieu, asked for Will. Will appeared shortly and invited Cliff to come in. The grocer refused and said, "No, really, Will, I'm not here on a social call. I just thought you ought to know that Grandpa Murray is sitting in the open window upstairs with his bare butt showing out of the window. Looks mighty strange to those passing by."

Will drew in a deep breath, and his eyes bulged. "Thank you, Cliff," he muttered, as he closed the door abruptly. "This is it! This is the last straw!" Will took the stairs two at a time and charged into Grandpa's bedroom. And there Michael sat in the window, stark naked. "You old fool," Will blurted out as he grabbed the old man by both shoulders and shook him violently. "You're driving us all crazy, Grandpa. I could kill you for this!"

In the midst of the commotion, Madeline appeared in the doorway, and when she saw Papa, her eyes filled with tears. "What are we going to do, Will?" she sobbed.

Shortly after that incident, Dan became ill and was confined to bed. With Dan in the house, Grandpa's behavior improved. But the improvement was short-lived: Dan had been diagnosed with cancer. It had all started with a badly decayed tooth a few months earlier. Dan had come home from work one night with an excruciating pain in his jaw.

"You have to see a dentist, Dan," Madeline pleaded. "Your face is badly swollen."

Dan responded plaintively, "Just get me some alum. That and a little whiskey should take the edge off the pain."

Dan waited a couple of months before boarding a streetcar to the doctor's downtown office, but it was too late. His cheek was rotting away, and the stench was so offensive that Madeline could hardly stand to be in his room. She cared for him at home, however, for several weeks. Finally Dan was hospitalized. He died shortly after that of starvation and the ravages of the disease.

After Dan's death, Grandpa spent most of his time sitting in a straight-backed rocker beside the newly acquired RCA radio, smoking his corncob pipe, listening to anything or sometimes nothing at all. Other times he played a haunting tune on his harmonica. One morning Baby Mary, only nine months old, crawling near Grandpa's chair in the parlor, discovered the key of an old clock on the floor. Instinctively, she put the key into her mouth and then began to cough and choke. After a minute or two, she slumped over onto the parlor floor.

"Madeline, for Christ's sake get in here! Something's wrong with the baby!" Michael hollered to Madeline, who was folding diapers on the kitchen table. Madeline came running; seeing her child turning blue, she grabbed Mary into her arms.

"Grandpa, what have you done to her?" Madeline screamed at the old man as she ran from the room. In sheer panic, she raced out of the back door to her neighbor, Laura Gaulke, and thrust the child into her arms. "She's dying, Laura! What can we do?"

The distraught mother shook with fear. Laura grabbed the limp and lifeless child, turned her upside down and pounded her back repeatedly. In seconds, a small sculptured key, hot and bloody, fell onto the floor. The baby sputtered, vomited and then slowly regained consciousness. Madeline wept in her friend's arms as the two of them held the baby close and swayed back and forth in a singular motion, their hearts and bodies entwined. Nobody ever knew for sure if Grandpa had dropped the key, but he was under suspicion for a long time.

Madeline's nerves were fraying and her patience grew thin. Will had trouble sleeping, and he found it difficult to concentrate on his new job for the Prudential Insurance Company. "I find myself falling asleep at my desk, Madeline, and I'm not very effective with the clients when I can't remember their names. Somehow we've got to find a way to get some sleep and some peace around here."

The two younger children often had respiratory problems, and Grandpa wandered around in his sleep, thinking he was back at the Murray farm. To make matters worse, the family had little in the cupboards to eat. Madeline planted a huge garden in the back yard in order to keep food on the table, but its care, along with the three children and her father, tasked her. Life was becoming an overwhelming challenge, and the children suffered the most.

Baby Mary contracted pneumonia during the winter and was confined to a steam tent for several days. Her condition critical, Will spent the nights kneeling by her crib administering the only antibiotic available in those days, his fervent prayers that God would spare his precious child. The older daughter, RoseAnn, developed bronchitis, and her chronic wheezing and coughing only added to the nightly drama.

Madeline and Will tried to spend a few precious moments alone between ministering to sick children and answering Grandpa's calls for help. When they did find time together, their treasured moments always tasted bittersweet. They had a fourth child on the way now, and they knew they could not afford another baby. In their youthful ardor, they had conceived four children in a little over seven years. Their problems were multiplying relentlessly.

After Christmas in 1932, Grandpa Murray's health began to fail. During the day, he stayed in bed and slept most of the time. At night, he ranted and raved, calling out for Rosanna, waking the children and sometimes falling down the stairs. On May 16, 1933, he died in his sleep of congestive heart failure. He was eighty-seven years old. Madeline arranged his funeral at the church in St. Martin, where he was buried beside Rosanna. A four-year nightmare had finally ended for Madeline and Will.

Chapter Six
A Matter of Ethics

THE GREAT DEPRESSION HAD REACHED a new low in 1933. As far back as Rosanna's death, prices for wheat and corn had been declining for farmers. By the time Grandpa Murray died, many people in the country were poverty-stricken. Madeline had been hopeful that she might be included in Grandpa's will, but as a foster child, she was not considered a legal heir, so economic hardships continued for the Matthews family. After the house on Seventeenth was sold, Madeline and Will rented another house next to Highway 52 on the west end of St. Cloud. Though a larger house, it had no domestic frills. Madeline again planted a garden in the back yard and sewed simple garments for the children.

Will continued to work for the Prudential Insurance Company, but he found it harder and harder to sell policies and to collect premiums from his policyholders. People just didn't have much money. During his third year at

Prudential, Will Matthews found himself in a dilemma. The manager, Pat Malley, had been carrying on a clandestine relationship with a secretary in the office for some time. Everyone in the office knew about it, but nobody said a word. Jobs were very scarce. One morning, Pat Malley called Will into his office supposedly for a job review.

"Bill," he said, "I see where your accounts are down this month. Would you like some help with canvassing? It's tough out there, I know." He patted Will on the shoulder.

"That's very kind of you, Mr. Malley. It is becoming dog-eat-dog, and I do have six hungry mouths to feed. I know you're a wonderful salesman; maybe you could teach me a thing or two. I'd be much obliged, sir."

Pat Malley's smile broadened, and then his demeanor sobered. "Now there's one little thing you could do for me, Bill," he began slowly. "Y'see, some of the big fellas in the home office have this idea that I'm being too friendly with Maureen. I don't know where they got that idea. Anyway, I need someone in our office to straighten them out, tell 'em there's absolutely no hanky-panky going on around here."

Will's heart sank.

Pat continued, "That's where you come in, Bill. I need you to vouch for me, sign a little paper to that effect."

Will knew what that meant: he had to lie for Pat Malley or he would lose his job.

Pat continued, "I'll have the paper ready for you tomorrow morning, my friend. I knew I could count on you, Bill." He gave Will no chance to object and promised to accompany him on his territory the following week.

That evening when the children were in bed, Will begged Madeline to sit with him for a few minutes to talk. Reluctantly, she put down her iron and sat on the sofa with her husband. Will leaned forward, his hands cupping his knees, his head bowed in grief. "Madeline, I'm in a tight spot at work," he said, "and I don't know what to do. We need the money, and I might lose my job." He hesitated then and waited for some reaction from his wife.

The color drained from Madeline's face. "Oh, Will, you can't lose your job. We have so many obligations, and winter is coming."

"Pat Malley wants me to lie for him on an affidavit, Madeline, and I don't think I can do that." Will continued, as he took his wife's hand, tears welling in his eyes. "I just can't, Madeline, and he'll fire me. I know he will."

Then Will explained that Pat was a married man with two children, yet he was involved with his secretary. The Prudential Insurance Company knew about it and was furious. Madeline stared at the floor for a long while. Finally, she looked up at Will and sighed, "Do what you have to do, Will."

Pat Malley promptly fired Will Matthews the next morning, leaving the fledgling salesman with a grieving wife, four hungry children, and a gaping wound in his heart. Will tried for weeks to find another job. The pantry shelves were growing empty. Only a few jars of canned tomatoes, a bag of flour, some dried hazelnuts, and a can of lard remained. That was all: no milk for the children, no eggs for pancakes, no meat or potatoes. Madeline was grateful when the neighborhood grocer gave her a limited credit account until the garden would come due again or Will would find a job.

In November, Will finally applied for a job with the Work Projects Administration and was placed at the St. Cloud Public Library mending books. The W.P.A. supported many people in the United States with a monthly stipend to help them survive the Depression. Will and Madeline were no exception.

For the Matthews children, school became a source of daily solace and times of great satisfaction. LeRoy, now in the third grade, had become a bright and promising student. He also found a job after school delivering the *Saturday Evening Post* in an effort to help out at home. RoseAnn, in the second grade, loved her teacher and found that reading opened up a world of excitement for her. Mary had started kindergarten, and her teacher, Miss Henke, praised her efforts at making up little rhyming jingles: "Apples are red, lemons are yellow. But I don't like either; I'd rather have Jello." Baby Maxine stayed at home with Madeline. In 1934 as the Depression continued, the joy and diversion of school helped the children to survive.

The Depression brought some interesting moments to the Matthews home, as well as difficulties. Beggars hitchhiking along Highway 52 routinely knocked on Madeline's door for a handout. "We're starving, ma'am," they complained. "Could you spare a sandwich or a donut or a cup of coffee?" Madeline obliged out of fear and compassion. She knew what it was like to be poor and homeless. But she also knew that Will would scold her when he got home for opening the door to the beggars. In her own defense, Madeline always had the same explanation: "When I'm here alone, Will, I think it's better to give them something to eat. Otherwise, they might force their way in and harm us. This way they just sit on the back steps for a while, eat their sandwich and leave." Will agreed that she was probably right. *After all,* he reminded himself, *the Depression has made beggars of everyone.*

In June 1935, another baby arrived for Madeline and Will. They welcomed their beautiful little daughter Kathleen but felt guilty for bringing her into a deprived and struggling world. Madeline nursed Kathleen for almost two years because there was no milk for the children, and already Maxine's tiny legs showed signs of rickets.

Mary, in the second grade at Garfield School, found it difficult, indeed, to keep up with Will and her older brother and sister as the four trudged the mile and one-half through rain and snow to Garfield School. Will tried to shield Mary from the blustery snow and cold with his long, black winter coat, but foot-deep snow often reached above the child's overshoes. Will had to carry her for blocks. After leaving the children at school, Will continued on another mile to the library, where he seldom missed a day. He found the work there demeaning, but at least the family could eat, and he could pay the monthly rent. For Will the long walk did not pose a major problem, but for the children it was a hardship.

The Matthews children could easily have attended a parochial school five blocks from their house, but the classes there had fifty students or more in each room. Madeline was adamant in her objection when Will proposed the idea. Her children were going to receive the best education available, and seventeen to twenty students per class at Garfield made much more sense to Madeline, long walk or not. "It's important, Will," she said again and again. "They have to get a good education."

Will reminded his wife of the pastor's warning at church on Sundays. "If you don't send your children to the church's school, you risk the danger of hell fire."

Madeline remained resolute, and the children continued at the public school.

At Garfield School the Matthews children not only excelled in reading, writing, and arithmetic, they were good in sports, too. At the annual District Field Day in late May of 1936, Lee was crowned the marbles champion, RoseAnn won the jump rope contest, and Mary took honors in hopscotch. On witnessing their successes, Madeline made a mental note to make their favorite chocolate cake for supper.

One of the teachers at the Field Day approached Madeline as she left the bleachers. "Mrs. Matthews," she said, "you must feed your children something very special to make them so agile and determined at school."

Madeline replied, "No, Miss Preus, I think it's the daily bottle of milk they receive here at school that makes the difference."

Miss Preus chuckled, thinking the answer was in jest.

Life turned somewhat brighter for Will and Madeline at Christmas that year. Lee was contributing five dollars a month to the family from his magazine delivery route, Will's stipend for his library work had been increased, and Madeline had taken in a roomer. The additional twenty-five dollars was a lot of money in 1936.

The young roomer worked at the gasoline station just down the highway and was delighted to find a room close by. He was almost twenty years old, and the children found him fascinating, especially his magic tricks. They didn't seem to mind bunching up in a bedroom to make room for Bernard.

For Christmas, Will bought a seven-foot balsam fir tree from the lot at Bernard's station and trimmed the magnificent tree with hundreds of multi-colored lights. There were few gifts, but Madeline played "Silent Night" on Rosanna's Hamilton piano, and the entire family felt blessed.

For diversion on late winter weekends, Madeline and Will spent Saturday evenings playing 500 with Madeline's childhood friend Rose and her husband Matt, who lived in nearby Waite Park. After cards, the foursome would have a piece of pie and a cup of coffee and talk politics. Matt, a confirmed conservative, had become a devout follower of Father Charles Coughlin, the anti-Roosevelt radical who advocated his own system of social justice and complete isolationism for the United States. Will tried hard not to argue with Matt for the sake of their friendship; but he and

Madeline were staunch Roosevelt supporters, and that made the situation difficult. Madeline always warned Will before their friends arrived not to push the politics too far, but the warning usually went unheeded. As he and Madeline undressed for bed, Will could be heard shouting angrily, "If it weren't for Rose, I'd throw him out. Next time invite Matt and Olive Keller. I hate the way Matt plays cards, but at least he's a Democrat."

Chapter Seven
Flying on the Wings of Faith

A TURN-OF-THE-CENTURY BABY, Will Matthews turned thirty-seven on March 14, 1937. "I'll never have trouble remembering how old I am," he joked to Madeline every year on his birthday. Will's hairline had receded, and he needed to wear his glasses, but he cut a handsome figure. The trials of family life had deepened the crow's feet between his bushy black eyebrows, but he still knew how to smile and be grateful. Placing one of his four small daughters on the toes of his shoes, he often danced around the house to the radio music of Guy Lombardo. "What a beautiful family we have, Madeline. God has blessed us in many ways."

Will was a deeply religious man. At six-thirty each morning, he walked to Mass at nearby St. Anthony's Church. He felt it important to stay in touch with the Lord and ask for God's blessing on the day. This daily contact with his God influenced Will's daily life. When he was still with Prudential, many of his policy holders were too poor to pay their weekly ten-cent premiums, and Will waived the premium for them and paid it himself or at least brought them a loaf of bread; though, Lord knows, bread was needed at home.

Occasionally, he spent a quarter on himself too, bringing home a brand new tie. Madeline chastised him for this. Watching him adjust his tie in the mirror before church on Sunday, she scolded, "Will Matthews, is that another new tie? You could buy a couple gallons of milk for that, you know." Feeling guilty, Will responded, "Yes, dear, never again." So it went until the next time.

Will possessed an inner faith in his God that buoyed his spirits in spite of hardship and motivated him to take care of both his physical and spiritual needs. Even the women who came to help when Madeline delivered her babies took a shine to Will, admiring his good looks and his buoyant smile.

On September 12, 1937, Will arrived home from work with a pain in his stomach. He couldn't eat supper and spent the evening on the daybed at the end of the dining room. By seven o'clock, his pain had increased. "Madeline, I think there is something wrong inside. Maybe you should call Dr. Halstrom."

"Is it that bad, Will? His house calls are very expensive." Then, noting the anguish in her husband's face, she ran to the telephone to make the call. "Doctor, please come to see Will. He's acting very strangely. I wouldn't call you out, but I'm really frightened."

Dr. Halstrom came shortly. "It's probably indigestion or constipation, Will. Try taking an enema before you go to bed," he suggested. Then he checked Will's abdomen one more time before he left.

By eight-thirty, Will was rolling back and forth on the floor. Madeline sent the children to bed and called Dr. Halstrom again. "It's serious, Doctor," she cried. "Will's getting worse. Please come out again."

The doctor listened and, noting the panic in Madeline's voice, agreed. "I'll be there in twenty minutes, Madeline," he promised, "and I'll bring my partner, Dr. Logan, with me."

The two doctors arrived in half an hour. In sharp contrast to tall, dark Dr. Halstrom, Dr. Logan was a short, red-haired man with large spectacles lodged half way down his nose. His baggy pants and tweed jacket looked as if he routinely lived in them. Alarmed at seeing Will on the floor in a fetal position groaning in pain, Dr. Logan knelt beside the patient and touched his belly lightly. Will cried out, "Please, Doctor, don't . . ."

Dr. Logan rose, turned to his partner and made his diagnosis: "It's appendicitis, Phil. We have to get him to the hospital."

Will's appendix ruptured as the doctor tried to remove it that night, and poison spread throughout his abdomen. Will Matthews died at the St. Cloud Hospital five days later, about six o'clock on a Sunday morning in late September. Peritonitis had set in, and, with no antibiotics to kill the infection, he had little chance of survival. A blood clot had also formed after surgery, which traveled to his brain and killed him. On a small slip of paper, Will scrawled his last message to his family: "Children, always be good to your mother." Madeline sobbed hysterically when she read the note. "Where is the God that Will believed in so ardently and served so faithfully? How can I tell the children that their precious daddy is gone forever."

The funeral brought a huge throng of mourners to the Matthews' home. Will had been laid out in the family living room where the rosary was recited for the repose of his soul. Mourners formed lines from the living room to the front sidewalk and half way down the block. They loved and respected this generous man who tried so hard to share himself and his limited resources with others. Observing the crowd, Madeline and her children began to realize how very dear Will was to many people, including many Prudential clients whose lives he had touched with his kindness.

Madeline's relatives and friends tried to console her with explanations, such as "The good always die first" and "Life is never fair," but these platitudes seemed meaningless to the distraught mother. Misguided efforts to keep the children away from Madeline so she could grieve in private were also not appreciated; her children were her only source of consolation.

After the funeral, on the day Will's two older brothers from Midland, Michigan, left to return home, Madeline gathered her family together. Two-year-old Kathleen sat on her mother's lap, as Madeline tried to explain to her sad and bewildered children that their daddy was now in heaven, and they would have to get along without him.

"I'll get a paper route," twelve-year-old LeRoy offered. "I can earn lots of money doing that, Mom, and with my Christmas tips too."

"And I'll help you with the work at home, Mom," said eleven-year-old RoseAnn. "I love to clean up the house."

"I'll take care of my little sisters," added eight-year-old Mary. "Maybe then you can sell insurance like Daddy, Mom."

Struggling to keep her composure, Madeline drew the children into her arms and held them close to her. "We'll be all right, children," she promised. "God will help us." Bleak as the future looked, Madeline had already made up her mind that her family would not lack for a good home.

During the first year, there were many adjustments to make. Madeline rented out a large room on the second floor of her home to three sisters who had just moved to St. Cloud from northern Minnesota: Merle, Tip, and Helen. She also reluctantly accepted Child Welfare payments to keep food on the table and pay the rent. But a voice inside of her kept telling her there was another way to cope if only she had the courage.

In the spring of 1939, when Mrs. Wilson, the regional welfare worker, made her bi-monthly visit to check on the children, she informed Madeline that there were certain rules that had to be observed. "First, you will not be allowed to own a car. Second, your children's progress in school will be monitored periodically. And third, the welfare monies must be used for necessities only — no frills, you understand. So keep a strict record of payments, which I can review when I come." The woman's tone was authoritative and demeaning. Madeline, who was used to handling her own affairs regardless of her financial status, resented the implication that she was incapable of taking care of her family, and that voice inside of her grew louder and louder.

In a sudden, unpremeditated outburst, Madeline shot back at the welfare worker, "Take your money, Mrs. Wilson. I'll make my own way! And please leave so I can tend to my children."

In dismay, Irene Wilson picked up her belongings and hurried out of the house, leaving Madeline with the sudden realization that she had just cut off the hand that had been feeding her and her five fatherless children.

The very next day Madeline unfolded one of the newspapers that LeRoy delivered and checked the Help Wanted section. At the bottom of the first column, she found an item of interest: "Ambitious, dedicated sales representative needed for the St. Cloud area. Apply to North American Life and Casualty Company district manager Henry Haugen, 409 Granite Exchange Bldg., St. Cloud, Minn." Madeline thought to herself: Doesn't say women can't apply. No salary mentioned. What would I do about the children? Well, at least I know a little about insurance from Will's work at Prudential. Isn't this what Mary thought I should do?

Madeline's heart pounded as she looked up the Henry Haugen's office phone number and repeated it to the operator. If she waited, she knew she would lose her nerve. She had to start somewhere, and she was determined that the children would not starve. The next morning she hopped an early bus for Henry Haugen's office.

Henry Haugen, a tall, heavy-boned Swede, had a heart as big as his stomach. He met with Madeline in his small, sparsely furnished office on the fourth floor of the Granite Exchange Building in downtown St. Cloud. Dressed in her black mourning dress with the white pointed collars, Madeline appeared in his doorway with a strained but determined look on her face.

"Come in, Mrs. Matthews," he greeted her. "I'm Henry Haugen. Won't you have a chair."

Madeline moved cautiously into the room and took a chair in front of Mr. Haugen's mahogany desk. This was the most difficult thing she had done since Will's death, but she had to try, and she had to succeed.

Side-stepping the high-backed swivel chair behind his desk, Henry Haugen sat down next to Madeline and threw one long leg over the other. "You sounded quite interested in my ad when you called yesterday," he said, with a congenial smile. "I like that kind of enthusiasm."

Madeline returned the smile and nodded, not knowing exactly how to respond.

"Do you have any experience in insurance work? Or in office work of any kind?" Henry continued, breathing audibly between questions.

"Not exactly, Mr. Haugen," Madeline confessed. "But my husband worked for Prudential Insurance before he died, and I used to help him with his bookwork. I am familiar with the insurance business. And I'm a fast learner." This she added quickly, trying to support her only real qualification.

"Well, I'm interested in someone I can train from scratch," said Henry. "I don't like having to un-train people with bad sales habits. And I like your attitude, Madeline. May I call you Madeline?"

"Oh, please do," said Madeline, eager to agree with anything Mr. Haugen had to say. "I have five children, you see, so I need a job, and I'll work very hard."

Henry Haugen sent Madeline to insurance school in Milwaukee to learn about a new form of insurance called hospitalization insurance, which was a sort of new kid on the block. The three sisters living upstairs agreed to look after the children for a week while Madeline was gone, allowing the anxious widow to travel with a fellow recruit to Milwaukee to begin her new career.

Impressed by Madeline's motivation and her grasp of the business, Henry spent many hours with his aspiring agent instructing her in details and having her accompany him on sales calls. Henry and his wife became so fond of Madeline that they invited the whole Matthews family to their Lower Town home for dinner on the occasion of her first anniversary with North American Life and Casualty.

Madeline's work called for a lot of changes. She set up her appointments primarily between 4:00 and 5:30 P.M.

and from 7:00 to 9:00 P.M., with an hour and one-half off for supper with the children. During these hours, men often had returned home from work, and LeRoy and RoseAnn, now fourteen and thirteen, could take care of the younger children. Madeline bought a car through an old friend from St. Martin who was working at Zapp Bank and was able to arrange a loan for her.

Her job called for other lifestyle changes, too—new clothes, cosmetics, and, most important of all, a facility to work well with other people. The ability to accept both success and failure were difficult at first, but she soon learned how to deal gracefully with either outcome. Her reward for a difficult evening's work was the sight of her five children grinning like Cheshire cats as she announced another policy sold. The children could actually tell by the look on their mother's face as she entered the door whether or not she had made a sale. Success meant a tremendous hug for her five cheerleaders, and a "no sale" brought a deep sigh and a prediction that tomorrow would be a better day.

Before long the smiles and hugs outnumbered the frowns and sighs as Madeline's business grew. The fact that nearly everyone eagerly welcomed the new concept of health insurance was a real boon, and commissions mounted steadily. Madeline herself became intrigued by her own success. She cautiously began to buy business suits, hats, high heels, and simple jewelry. If only Michael and Rosanna, and especially Will, could see her now. She hoped they would be proud of her as she drove her own car on the way to a promising prospect.

By the fall of 1940, with all of her children in school, Madeline could spend more time advancing her business career. She usually cleaned the house in the morning after the children left for school and then started her telephone calls to set up late afternoon and evening appointments. Most of her prospects came from policyholders thrilled to have their hospital bills paid from a source other than their own wallets, though they still had to pay for office calls. These prospect names Madeline wrote into her all-important appointment book, which she kept in a small briefcase in her bedroom away from the sticky fingers of her five inquisitive children.

On a typical day, Madeline changed into a business suit about 3:30 P.M., applied some powder on her nose and a little color to her lips and prepared to step into the business world. Through her bedroom window, she sometimes saw Lou Walbridge, her next door neighbor, returning from her Auction bridge group. Staring out of the window, Madeline would muse about the difference in their lives: *I know Lou admires me for working, but I think she feels sorry for me, too. Sometime I'd like to tell her "Lou, don't pity me. I love what I'm doing, and I love all the interesting people I meet everyday." Maybe that's why I was lonely on the Murray farm. And I love the challenge, too.* Then speaking more directly to the figure outside her window, she concluded: *You might be interested to know, Lou, that I'm not lonely anymore.* With that thought in mind, Madeline zipped up her briefcase, picked up her car keys and headed down the steps to the front door.

After two years of progress in the work force, Madeline moved her family to a new and better neighborhood on the south side of town, and Helen, one of her roomers, asked to come along. Helen's sisters had married, and she now felt like one of Madeline's family. Madeline was overjoyed because Helen was often at home in the evening when she had to go out on appointments. It was a good arrangement for everyone.

Helen's boyfriend, Baron, often visited in the evening and became a friend to the children, just as Bernard had done several years earlier. One evening after Maxine and Kathleen had gone to bed, RoseAnn and Mary hid at the top of the staircase in complete darkness and watched intently as Helen and Baron talked, then fell into each other's arms on the living room sofa. Their kisses lasted so long that the two young eavesdroppers looked questioningly at each other and wondered what was going to happen next. Helen suddenly broke into tears and held Baron at arm's length. "But you might be killed, sweetheart. I don't want you to be killed."

"I don't have much choice, Angel. I'm in a bind. It's either be drafted or join the marines."

"Then wait and be drafted," Helen demanded. And so he did, and he was, in about six months. World War II was beginning, and it, like the Great Depression, changed the lives of many Americans.

Madeline's boss, Henry Haugen, retired and left St. Cloud in 1942. The district manager of North American Life and Casualty from Minneapolis took over the St.

Cloud area and became Madeline's supervisor. He stopped regularly to visit and helped Madeline with wavering prospects. His name was John Grey.

At first the relationship was completely business-oriented, but after a few months, John Grey's interest in Madeline became more than platonic. He began to notice her bright green eyes, her neatly styled chestnut hair, and the soft, generous curves of her body. Routinely, he asked her to have dinner with him to discuss business prospects or to have a drink with him before he left town. St. Cloud became a weekly stop on John's business circuit. Madeline was flattered by his attention, and John's invitations to movies and fancy restaurants offered exciting new experiences for her. However, as the relationship grew, Madeline realized the seriousness of John Grey's intentions.

"We're a good pair, Madeline," John began one Friday evening after dinner. "And I really like the kids. I think they like me, too. Don't you think so?"

Madeline felt a familiar fluttering in her stomach and a sudden urge to move away from John, who had reached out to hold her hand. She didn't like the direction the conversation seemed to be taking. What was he thinking? That she might marry him? Oh, no! She must have given him a wrong impression. She still loved Will. And the children—they were not ready to accept a new father. How could she make John understand? He had done so much for her, but she wanted only to be friends. He was looking at her in a new and different light now, and it made her feel very uncomfortable.

"John, please wait: I need to tell you something." Groping for words, she began, "You are my dear friend, John . . . but I'm not interested in any commitment. Can't we just continue as we are?" Madeline's voice and her whole demeanor pleaded for understanding.

John hesitated and then smiled. "Of course, Madeline. I didn't mean to pressure you. It's probably too soon for you even to think about a serious relationship." Then he added slowly and thoughtfully, but with a note of finality in his voice, "I'll always be your friend."

Madeline's children had always been the jewels in her crown. With Will gone now, her love and concern for them seemed sufficient to make her life meaningful and rewarding. She treasured John's friendship, but that would have to suffice.

That night Madeline tossed restlessly in bed, and sleep would not come. She tried sucking in long, deep breaths and exhaling slowly to the count of ten, but that didn't work. Then she counted a few sheep, but they turned into soldiers jumping over barbed wire fences. No doubt the war broadcasts on the radio infiltrated her thoughts. Would the Nazis bomb the United States? How would the war affect her family? Then she began to wonder why she had rejected John when he could have offered her such material comfort and security. Will was gone, and when the children left, she would be alone. Her answer came quickly: she didn't love John, and it would be wrong to marry him for her own selfish purposes. No, she had done the right thing. She would hold on to every precious moment with her children and then deal with whatever came next. "Just give me a clue, Lord, when that time comes: tell me again which way to go." Madeline stretched long and hard, her heels making deep grooves in the soft, wind-dried sheets. Then she turned over on her side, punched her pillow and fell asleep.

John's visits reverted to a monthly basis after that, and any sense of urgency vanished.

Chapter Eight
Letting Go

PRESIDENT ROOSEVELT HAD CALLED December 7, 1941 "a day of infamy," but in many respects, World War II brought out the best in Americans. Young men and women eagerly volunteered to fight the good fight to defeat Adolf Hitler, and everyone worked together to achieve the common goal of victory over tyranny. Rationing brought a sudden awareness of the real quality of life in America; and, most important, the wartime economy produced millions of lucrative jobs for people who had been out of work during the Depression years. Women, in particular, could pursue occupations outside of the home that never before had been open to them. "Rosie, the Riveter" became a national theme song, and the liberation of women in America gained momentum.

Madeline and her family experienced both the advantages and sacrifices of the booming wartime economy. As men went off to war and women took their places, Madeline was no longer a rarity in the business world. Eager to advance in her career and having learned the intricacies of the insurance business, she found herself intrigued by investments and securities. The John G. Kinnard Investment Company offered her an opportunity to join their local team.

Madeline's career advanced rapidly with the help of family and friends. Her children were growing up and could stay by themselves when necessary, and Madeline was free to make daytime as well as evening appointments. When she arrived home, she brought steak or pork chops for supper, instead of dishing up tuna or hamburger casseroles several times a week. Lee, a junior at Cathedral High School, maintained an "A" average and worked part time as a draftsman at the Kollmann Monumental Company. At sixteen, RoseAnn had a job as a sales clerk at J.C. Penney on Saturdays, and Mary took care of her younger sisters at home and tried her hand at cooking. The war forced everyone to take on added responsibilities, and Madeline and her children were no exception.

In the fall of 1943, in Lee's senior year in high school, a United States Navy recruiter visited Cathedral High School to speak to the senior boys about enlisting in the Navy after graduation. He stressed that the government offered a program whereby veterans could go to college free of charge. This program could help students like Lee, who worried about how to pursue a college career.

Lee approached his mother one Friday evening after she returned home from an appointment. "Mom, we need to talk," he said, with a note of urgency in his voice. "Let's go to my bedroom where it's quiet." Madeline immediately sensed some kind of major announcement. "I heard about a wonderful opportunity the other day, Mom, for me to go to college free, and I'm really excited about it." The words spilled out of Lee's mouth.

An ominous feeling swept over Madeline. "Slow down, son. Where did you get an idea like that?"

"Well, a Navy recruiter came to school the other day to talk to the guys about enlisting after graduation. He said the Navy had a special V-12 program where you could go to school while serving in the Navy. I would have to repay the government with periods of active duty, but I wouldn't mind that. Just think of the opportunity I would have. It would be a great deal for me, Mom! Maybe I could even go to medical school that way if I did a good job."

Madeline knew that her son had his heart set on becoming a doctor and that this program must have sounded like the chance of a lifetime. He seemed so excited. Lee continued to expound, hardly stopping for air. "I know this would be hard on you, Mom, but I'll probably be drafted anyway if I don't do something like this. So what do you think? Should I look into it? Lots of my buddies say they're going to sign up with the Navy rather than be drafted."

Madeline just stared at the bedroom wall. She remembered how helpful her son had been since Will's death. That first Christmas he had put up the Christmas tree and bought presents for everyone with the tips from his paper route. Then he had helped her with expenses by working off his tuition and that of his sisters when Madeline made the decision to send her children to Cathedral High School, a private school with an excellent reputation for college preparation. Lee had been a father figure for his sisters and a source of strength for her. Now he wanted to leave them all to join the Navy.

Madeline's first inclination was to say, "No, son, I need you at home. Maybe they won't even draft you since you help to support your family. You just can't leave us yet." But those words stuck in her throat. Instead, she suggested a grace period. "Just let me think about it, Lee. You've dropped a big bombshell."

"Sure, Mom," Lee replied. "But think fast. I don't have much time to decide."

Madeline retreated to the living room and sat in the old mahogany rocker she had salvaged from the Murray farm so many years before and picked up her crochet project from the table beside it. This was a relaxing pastime that Rosanna had taught her, and it often drove away the demons for a while. However, Madeline could think of nothing but her son's plan after that. It haunted her like a bad dream. Just when her life had taken on meaning again and she felt secure with her job and her family, a cloud had formed on the horizon. On the other hand, she wondered if she could forgive herself if she deprived her son of this chance. She couldn't keep her son tied to her forever; she had to let go. God would help her again, and she had her four daughters who were very dear to her.

When Madeline gave Lee the good news on Sunday evening, he was overjoyed. "Son, you have my blessing on your new adventure if you want to pursue it. I'll help you in any way I can."

Not believing his ears, Lee jumped to his feet and hugged his mother passionately. "Oh, Mom, you mean it? Really, you don't mind? I'll never forget you for this, Mom. Truly, I won't. And I promise I'll always be here for you when you need me, even if I'm a thousand miles away." The young man was exuberant, and he lay awake half the night imagining himself in an operating room saving the life of someone like his dad. It was the beginning of a new chapter in his life and in Madeline's, too.

Lee graduated as salutatorian of his class at Cathedral in the spring of 1943. In January he had picked up the credits in German needed to qualify for the Navy's V-12 pre-medical program. To Madeline's surprise, it was Father Val Mondloch from St. Martin who tutored Lee at St. John's University, and by August, he had completed a full year's credits. Lee was now prepared to leave for John Carroll University in Cleveland to begin his V-12 program with the Navy.

Life was not the same around the Matthews' home without Lee, though he wrote home every week sharing his new adventures with his mother and sisters. His letters were always a combination of humor and pathos.

In one letter, he wrote them about having dinner at the home of a beautiful girl he had met at a USO club in Cleveland. Her name was Betty Bond, and her father owned the famous Judy Bond Blouse Company. The dinner had been a traumatic event because the Bonds were extremely wealthy, and their dinner presented a frightening social challenge. The table setting alone made Lee's knees tremble: three forks on one side of the plate, two knives and three spoons on the other side. He had watched carefully as Betty's mother, a gracious, staid woman in her fifties, used a new piece of silver for each new item of food brought in by a server. Lee had never tasted any of the strange foods served: curried spinach salad, smoked salmon, broccoli au gratin. . . . His friend Betty identified the courses as subtly as she could, but that did not improve the taste for the young sailor who had never eaten gourmet food, much less in a dining room like this. Frustrated, Lee finally stacked up his unused silverware and politely excused himself, explaining that he was already late for his check-in time at the dorm. After that, he questioned his dance partners more carefully at the USO before accepting invitations to their homes. Lee ended his letter: "Gosh, Mom, I'd give my right arm for some of your pot roast and mashed potatoes," which brought a smile to Madeline's face. Lee's letters provided a diversion from the winter doldrums and were always the highlight of the week for Madeline and the girls.

After he finished two years of accelerated pre-medical studies at John Carroll, Lee was transferred in October 1944, to active duty at Sampson Naval Hospital in New York. There he helped to care for Navy men who had contracted tuberculosis in the line of duty. To his great dismay, one of his best friends developed tuberculosis in the process of working with the diseased seamen. The young sailor's name was Bill Tooker, and he and Lee remained friends all of their lives.

From his station at Sampson, Lee sent letters to his family recounting more unique and exciting experiences. Then, on a sultry July evening in 1945, a call for help came to Madeline from her panic-stricken son. "Mom, please, please don't ask me any questions, but could you possibly get two hundred dollars somewhere to send to me tomorrow morning. I need it right away, Mom, and I'll pay you back next month, I promise."

Madeline hesitated only momentarily. Lee obviously didn't want to tell her why he needed the money. But she had promised to help him in any way she could when he left for the Navy. With confidence in her son's integrity and judgment, she answered his call for help.

"I'll try, son. I'll talk to Mr. Zapp at the bank and see if I can borrow the money. Where should I send it?"

"Oh, thanks, Mom. I'll love you forever for helping me out," he promised. "Just wire it to me in care of Sampson Naval Station, Barracks #4. And thanks again, Mom. You're the best mother a guy ever had."

Madeline thought he sounded guilty about something, but her faith in him was absolute. She was his mother, and he needed help. The next morning Eddie Zapp lent her the money on a personal promissory note. She wired it immediately to her son no questions asked, no answers given. The matter remained a permanent family mystery.

Lee never lived in St. Cloud again, but he came home often to visit. From Sampson Naval Hospital, he was admitted to Harvard Medical School in Boston in October 1945. His sharp mind had not gone unnoticed by either John Carroll University or the Navy. At Harvard, he was a top honor student and also worked part time at the Huntington Street Laboratory. He married his high school sweetheart, "Rock," and they stayed in touch with Madeline by letter and by phone and helped her periodically with medical advice and financial support for special projects. Proud of her son's achievements, Madeline wished only that Will could have lived to see his son blossom into adulthood.

Chapter Nine
Letting Go, Part II

WHILE HER SON'S CAREER ADVANCED on the East Coast, Madeline coped with the problems of her four growing daughters at home. RoseAnn, in high school, had grown into a beauty with long, black hair, velvety brown eyes, and flawless complexion. She looked more like Will than any of the other children. In the bold colors she chose to wear, she stood out in a crowd, and her popularity in school continued to grow.

The incident that accounted for at least some of that popularity occurred when RoseAnn was a freshman member of the Cathedral High School Drum and Bugle Corps. Late one afternoon as the Corps practiced in the gym for the forthcoming Homecoming festivities, RoseAnn, drum on hip, had marched past another drummer in formation and snagged her skirt on the other girl's drum frame. The fragile snaps on her skirt placket gave way, and her skirt fell ceremoniously to the floor. Football and basketball players filled the bleachers, and when they saw the unfrocked drummer grab frantically for her skirt they whooped and hollered raucously. In utter shock and embarrassment, RoseAnn hoisted her skirt and ran tearfully to the nearest exit. When she arrived home from her practice, flustered and devastated, she ran sobbing to her mother, "Mom, I just can't go back to school again. Everyone will laugh and poke fun at me. I'll have to transfer to Tech." Then, as Madeline calmed her down, RoseAnn described the horrible incident and swore again that she would never go back to school.

Madeline had never faced this kind of problem before. Her daughter was hysterical and hurting terribly. Still, she said gently, "I know how embarrassed you must feel, dear, but this will blow over in a few days. After all, you didn't do anything wrong. Accidents happen all the time. I'm sure the boys' catcalls were just a spontaneous reaction to what seemed like a big joke to them."

She tried in vain to minimize the situation, but in RoseAnn's eyes she was marked for life. Madeline held her daughter close for several minutes and allowed her to cry. Madeline knew that a good cry was the best medicine for a multitude of problems. Then she took her daughter by the hand and led her to the kitchen. "I really need some help out here, honey. Could you set the table for me?"

When RoseAnn returned to school the next morning, there was a message in her homeroom to report to the principal's office. The bewildered freshman answered the sum-

mons only to find that Father Krebs was a very straightfor-
ward man, and his solution to the whole problem was just
to have a zipper put into her skirt. From then on, RoseAnn
was known as "Zip" at school, and her telephone never
stopped ringing.

As Lee entered Harvard in the fall of 1945, RoseAnn
continued as a day student at the College of St. Benedict in
St. Joseph. Her aim was to become a teacher, which had
always been Madeline's dream. By this time, Rosie, as she
was known then, had narrowed a long list of suitors to a
handsome, blond Marine who had been a star football
player at Tech and served in the Pacific theater of World
War II. Rosie had already completed three years at St. Ben's
when Ves came home from the war. He was an eager young
veteran—eager, that is, to put his gut-wrenching military
experience behind him and marry the beautiful girl about
whom he had dreamed for three long years in Iwa Jima,
Okinawa, and the Philippines.

The homecoming played like a scene from a
Hollywood movie. Ves, dashingly handsome in his Marine
uniform, rang the bell at Madeline's front door. And Rosie,
dressed in her black-and-white pleated skirt and a red
turtleneck sweater, could have passed for Linda Darnell, as
she answered the bell. They fell into each other's arms—
embracing, kissing and smiling, forgetting completely that
the whole family was watching.

Ves gave Rosie a lovely diamond ring for Christmas
in 1947, and the two young lovebirds seemed deliriously
happy. Madeline shared her daughter's joy, but she was

also concerned about RoseAnn's education. Surely, she wouldn't jeopardize her three highly successful years of college with talk of getting married.

Madeline confronted her daughter a few days after the New Year, "You're going to finish school, aren't you, RoseAnn? You can't just waste all the effort you've put into these last three years!"

RoseAnn listened politely but her answer sounded resolute, "I'm not going to waste anything, Mother, but Ves and I are getting married."

As it turned out, RoseAnn was offered a teaching job by the superintendent of the Melrose Public Schools without even completing her bachelor's degree. Teachers were in great demand in 1947, and state licensure was preferred but not required. RoseAnn taught for one year before her marriage, which allayed her mother's concerns. She and Ves married on June 10, 1948, at St. Mary's Cathedral in St. Cloud, and the wedding turned out picture perfect in every way.

As Madeline watched her beautiful daughter walk down the long middle aisle of the Cathedral on the arm of her brother Lee, she knew that this would be the story of the rest of her life, giving up her children. She missed Will so desperately at that moment her heart ached. Yet she knew she had to have courage for her other daughters' sakes. She prayed, "Give me strength, Lord, to finish the job Will and I started so many years ago."

Chapter Ten
Adventures of a Middle Child

"SISTER WAS VERY CONVINCING, MOM. She said we could do a lot of good for some poor kids and have a great adventure at the same time." Mary stood in the doorway of her mother's bedroom staring at the picture of her father on Madeline's nightstand. *If only Dad were here now, I'm sure he would let me go*, she thought. "Mary Ann and Rita want to go, Mom," she continued, referring to her two best friends. "Their parents said it's all right with them, so could you please give it some thought and let me know soon. I'll lose my chance if you don't decide quickly."

Seventeen-year-old Mary was giving her mother the same kind of ultimatum her brother had used three years earlier at just the same age. Instead of joining the Navy, Madeline's second oldest daughter wanted to go to a social service camp in California to be a counselor for most of the summer.

"The camp is run by the Sisters of Social Service in Los Angeles, Mother, and it's a very safe place in the San Bernadino Mountains." Mary had explained the circumstances to her mother before and had expected faster approval of her altruistic agenda to serve the slum kids from Los Angeles on the one hand and perhaps see Hollywood on the other. Mary knew that her mother did not make decisions regarding her children rashly, so she waited impatiently to hear her decision.

This discussion occurred in 1946, and, at that time, Madeline was still meeting professionally with John Grey, so she decided to discuss this latest ultimatum with him. After all, John was a man of the world, and he would be more familiar with California and the prospects for disaster there. All Madeline knew about California was that it was a long way from Minnesota and that the people there seemed to have a very different style of living.

"That would be an absolutely fabulous experience for Mary," John confided to Madeline when he heard about the young girl's plans. "She's a middle child, you know, and she needs to develop some confidence in her own abilities and judgment. And, really, Madeline, that area of California is breathtakingly beautiful. Why not let her go! She's a good girl, and it will help her to grow up."

The day after her meeting with John, Madeline summoned her daughter to the back porch out of earshot of her two younger sisters, who were peeling potatoes and chopping lettuce at the kitchen sink. Madeline didn't want Maxine and Kathy to get any premature ideas from their sister.

"I've given your California proposal a lot of thought, Mary." Madeline began with some trepidation in her voice. "I do have some reservations about three innocent girls traveling so far in a Greyhound bus without an adult. John seems to think that the experience would be good for you though, to help you grow up and allow you to experience a new and beautiful part of our country."

Madeline approached Mary and lovingly placed her hand on the girl's shoulder. "I've been afraid to let you go, Mary. You seem so young to leave home for such a long time. RoseAnn has never asked to do anything like this, and she's in college." Her words were not, however, conveying accurately the mixed feelings in her heart. There was a part of her that wanted to say, "Go, fly like a bird, my precious daughter. Fill your life with challenges. Go where your heart would take you, and don't let anyone break your spirit." But those words would not sound mature or responsible. Instead, she said, "Don't you think you might be getting ahead of yourself, Mary?"

"But, Mom," insisted Mary, "Rosie has Ves, and she doesn't want to do something like this. I do! Mary Ann and Rita and I will stick together like glue, and we'll be very careful. I promise!"

Madeline had to admit that Mary had always been a model student and a dependable child, and her spirit of adventure was enviable. At fifteen, she had found an after-school job at Kresge's and was still graduating as valedictorian of her class. She had good common sense, too, so why deny her this opportunity that meant so much to her.

"All right, young lady, you can go. But you must promise to write every week and share your experiences with us. Always remember, dear, how precious you are to your family." Madeline's heart pounded not only for having decided but because she knew how fortunate her daughter was to have this chance. If only Rosanna had given her that opportunity. Madeline's decision made an indelible impression on Mary, and she loved her mother deeply for her unselfish way of letting her children go.

The two thousand-mile trip to California by Greyhound bus provided an interesting but sometimes frightening experience for the three would-be counselors from Sister Gerard's Social Studies class at Cathedral. In Idaho Falls, Idaho, Mary was abandoned when she stayed too long in the ladies' room at the bus station. Several blocks down the road, Rita finally summoned enough courage to inform the bus driver that one of the passengers was missing. As he pulled the bus over to the curb to wait, in his rear view mirror, he saw Mary running frantically down the road after the disappearing bus.

Once at Camp Mariastella, the St. Cloud trio found themselves enthralled by the mountains, the streams, and even the rattlesnakes. The California mountains provided a completely new scene for three fledgling travelers who had grown up with prairies, pine trees, and cornfields. Mary filled her letters to her family with excitement: getting lost in the mountains on a Sunday afternoon hike, encountering a rattlesnake with the distinctive X's on its back enroute to the swimming hole, staying with the Sisters of Social

Service in a converted bishop's mansion in Los Angeles, visiting Hollywood on a weekend pass and, of course, trying to counsel disadvantaged twelve-year-olds from the inner city slums. That summer at Camp Mariastella in the California mountains became the first of Mary's adventures. Madeline could never deny the girl another learning experience.

In 1948, Mary took her first trip on a train to Boston where she lived for a year with her brother Lee and his new bride and attended Emmanuel College, which was just around the corner from Harvard Medical School.

The Sisters of Notre Dame da Namur conducted classes at Emmanuel College, and many of the students were from families of the Irish nouveau riche. Mary found them to be friendly, helpful, fun-loving girls but incredibly provincial. At a Western movie one evening, Sarah Sweeney, one of these girls, asked Mary in all sincerity whether people still hitched their horses to a post in St. Cloud. Katie Cavanaugh was extremely excited one morning because she was taking a trip out west. When Mary asked where she was going, Katie proudly announced, "to Springfield."

In one letter, Mary wrote, "Guess what, Mom? My best friend and I have been chosen to be hostesses at Emmanuel's night at the Boston Pops on the Esplanade along the Charles River. It's a great honor, Mom. I can hardly believe it." Other letters told of mastering the Boston subway system; working Saturdays in the marine department of Boston Insurance Company; dating a sophisticated store designer from the famous Jordan Marsh Company, who was originally from Freeport, Minnesota; and canoeing down the Charles River for a picnic with a debonair young man from Boston College—a memorable year, just as the summer in California had been. In just two years, Mary had traveled from the West Coast to the East Coast in a tremendous leap of faith and distance, all with her mother's blessing.

Chapter Eleven
The East Coast Pilgrimage

In June 1949, Madeline, too, traveled to Boston. She was unable to resist the opportunity to see her only son graduate from a prestigious medical school like Harvard. This was the fulfillment of a dream beyond her grandest expectations. Lee, the son of that little Murray girl who slept with the frost on her coverlets and had only a fifth grade education, was graduating third in his class from Harvard Medical School with an "M.D." attached to his name.

Her plane ride to Boston proceeded flawlessly, like a fairy tale. She had never flown anywhere; she had been happy just to have her temperamental two-door Willys for travel at home. Flying was for the rich. But Lee had sent her the money for her ticket from his earnings at the Huntington Street Lab, and she liked traveling on her own.

When Madeline arrived at Logan Airport in Boston, Lee and Mary met her at the gate. As she emerged from the plane, they observed her walking from the ramp to the gate. They noticed something different about their mother — the bounce in her step perhaps or the way she held her head high and smiled openly as she approached. She wore her new, navy-blue Pendleton suit with a white, tuxedo-front blouse and high heels. On her head, a white chiffon scarf protected her freshly styled hair from the wind. To her children, she was a petite fifty-two-year-old beauty, looking more like forty, who was making them feel very proud and excited. And, best of all, she was their mother.

Lee greeted his mother warmly, throwing his arms around her in an all-embracing hug. "Mom, you look wonderful. Did you have a good trip?"

Madeline returned her son's embrace. "It was quite an experience for me. My first flight!" Then she took Mary, who had been waiting to be noticed, into her arms. "Oh, Mary, we've missed you so. It seems you've been gone forever. We'll be happy to have you home again."

Two days later, with the impressive Harvard graduation ceremonies behind them, Madeline and her daughter left for New York City, this time by train. Their destination, the New York Foundling Hospital, 175 East Sixty-eighth Street, the place from which Madeline had come to Minnesota on the Orphan Train as a child. Lee had arranged this side trip for his mother because he knew that she had always wanted to know more about her birth parents and why they had given her up.

As their taxi approached the old brick and stone hospital, Madeline's stomach began to churn, and Mary instinctively put her arm around her mother and guided her up the steps to the hospital door. Madeline stopped abruptly and hesitated . . . then pushed the door open.

At the information desk inside, an elderly gray-haired woman greeted them with a smile. "What can I do for you, ladies?"

Madeline cleared her throat and answered, "We are looking for information on a child named Madeline McCarthy, who was sent to Minnesota on the Orphan Train back in 1899. Is it possible that there could still be records on her here?"

Mary added, "We want to find out about her parents. Can you help us?"

"Well, I don't know, but we can certainly try," replied the woman. "You will have to take the elevator to the basement level to the archives. As you leave the elevator, go down the first hall to the right. Look for the office marked Archives. I think the people there might be able to help you." As an afterthought, she added, "We actually have hundreds of people who come here every year seeking information on the Orphan Trains."

The archives proved to be a large room with shelves and shelves of old volumes containing records kept by the hospital for over one hundred years. Here interested parties might find records from the middle 1800s on the histo-

The New York Foundling Home from where many orphans, including Madeline, were sent to families in Stearns County, Minnesota.

ry of the foundling hospital and the children who had been residents there.

"How may I help you?" asked a tall, bearded, young man.

"We are looking for information on a child sent to Minnesota on one of the Orphan Trains about 1899. Do you have records from that far back?" Madeline did not identify herself.

"Are you related to this person, ma'am?" the man asked.

"Yes, I am this person," Madeline explained with a blush. "I'm Madeline McCarthy. I want to learn about my real parents."

"I see," said the man whose name badge read Christopher Dawson. "I'll be glad to look that name up for you. The older volumes are in another room. Please sit down. It shouldn't take long." He left and Madeline and her daughter sank into the designated chairs and stared at each other in silence.

When Christopher Dawson returned, he had a small note pad in hand. "I found the name Madeline McCarthy," he said and read from the note pad: "Two-year-old girl sent from this institution on October 20, 1899, on the Orphan Train to one Michael Murray in Minnesota. Parents: John McCarthy and Sarah Dougherty McCarthy (deceased), immigrants from Cork County, Ireland. Birth date: July 22, 1897. Race: Caucasian. Religion: Roman Catholic. Baptized by Rev. C.M. Thuente, O.P., after arrival at our hospital. That's about it," he concluded.

"Is there no information on why I was left at the foundling hospital? Were my parents dead *then* or did they die later?" asked Madeline, eager to glean as much knowledge from the skimpy information, to give some explanation of who she was and why she had been given away to strangers.

"I'm sorry, Mrs. . . ." the young man said, hesitating.

"My name is now Madeline Matthews," Madeline broke in, "and I'm sorry I didn't introduce my daughter. This is Mary. She accompanied me from Boston."

"I'm sorry I don't have more to tell you, Mrs. Matthews. You're luckier than most. Thousands of babies were left in our waiting rooms by poverty-stricken parents. Often there's no information whatever to give people."

Madeline forced a smile and thanked him for his time. They had heard nothing new in the information he had given her, and they could not accomplish more there. At least she had tried. There was a sense of closure for her even in that fruitless effort.

On returning to Minnesota, Madeline and Mary never mentioned the incident to anyone and rarely referred to it themselves. For Madeline, her life before the Murray farm was now a closed book, and she made no further attempts to re-open it. The old five-story, red-brick-and-stone New York Foundling Hospital at 175 East sixty-eighth Street in New York City was demolished in 1958, just nine years after Madeline's visit; and the operation moved to another location. Madeline seemed pleased that at least she had seen the origional historic site from which she had come to Minnesota in 1899.

Chapter Twelve
Downsizing Again

IN THE FALL OF 1949, MARY RETURNED to the College of St. Benedict to pursue an English major. Madeline was delighted to have her home again. After graduation in 1951, however, Mary discussed with her mother an offer she had received at school to take over a position in Washington, D.C., as office manager of the immigration bureau of the National Catholic Welfare Conference (NCWC).

"Lois Malachy is coming back here to enter the convent, Mom, and she thinks I would really enjoy working for Bruce Miller. He's the head of the bureau. I think working in Washington would be a fascinating experience. Maybe you could come to visit me sometime."

"Don't count on that, Mary. I have two other daughters who need their mother around to keep them in line. Remember how complicated life was when you were in high school? But I want you to go, Mary. The nation's capital is probably the most exciting and interesting place in the country. Besides that, Harry Truman could use a little help."

Mary left for Washington in early June. The work was interesting enough, but she faced some problems. For one thing, the weather in D.C. was abominable that summer — so hot and humid that Mary sometimes sat for hours in the evening on the fire escape outside her window to get a breath of fresh air. All she ever really got was the steam emanating from the lamplight outside her window. Other times she tried sitting in a tepid bath after work, imagining that she was enjoying a cool dip in a refreshing Minnesota lake. Air conditioning existed only in government buildings, and she could find no respite from the sweltering heat.

Another problem involved a more perplexing situation. One of the young priests at NCWC offered Mary a ride home after work one evening since he lived in the same suburb. Mary, lonely and somewhat naïve, never suspected an ulterior motive until her friend announced on the way home that they would be stopping off for dinner at Milligan's Restaurant. As he removed his Roman collar, he warned her, "For heaven's sake, don't call me 'Father.' Mark will be just fine." When this happened a second and third time, Mary became concerned and called her brother Lee for advice.

"What do you think about a young priest asking me out to dinner repeatedly, Lee? He's a wonderful person, but

I'm getting a little nervous about the whole thing. I need some advice, and I don't want to call Mom."

"Just relax," Lee advised. "He probably just enjoys a little female companionship. Don't be so judgmental. Priests are human, too, you know." It was easy for Lee to philosophize, but Mary continued to be concerned.

In late August, she called the Minnesota Department of Education to ask about openings for an English teacher for the fall term. She found one opening still available in Kensington, a small town where the famous Runestone had been discovered. "English nine, ten, eleven, and twelve," the personnel director told her matter-of-factly, "and you would be the librarian and gym teacher, as well." Without hesitation, Mary answered, "I'll take it." That decision led to an eighteen-year career in education and a romance with great potential.

Mary's teaching experience proved highly successful and fulfilling, but weekends in Kensington, a town of four hundred people, seemed dull, so she often went home to St. Cloud to visit her family. On an early October weekend with the leaves turning marvelous shades of red, orange, and purple, she just happened to meet an old high school classmate on a street corner near her home. He had been the president of the student council at Cathedral and had been voted the best citizen in the class. With his blond, curly hair, serious blue eyes and the stature of a West Pointer, he seemed more than a pleasant chance encounter. The two old friends stood on the corner chatting for a while, supposedly catching up on the past five years, but really eyeing each other appreciatively.

Ed had come home for a long weekend from Father Flanagan's Boystown in Omaha. After eighteen months in the Army, he had completed his degree in Social Work and Political Science at St. Louis University and was earning money to return to school for an advanced degree. Mary told him briefly about her all-inclusive position as an English teacher at Kensington High School and admitted that she looked forward to a three-month return trip to Washington, D.C., with two teacher friends. Ed said that he had a sister living in Washington and had been invited many times to visit her but was always too involved in his educational pursuits. Before parting, the two friends promised to keep in touch.

A month later, Mary received a letter addressed to her in care of Kensington High School. It had an Omaha postmark. Ed's letters at first seemed very serious, primarily concerned with some social injustice or world-shaking event and were signed "Just Ed." Mary wrote back that his sermons were so effective he really should be a priest. That comment must have struck a nerve because future letters became much more light-hearted and were signed "Love, Ed." Mary thought they were making progress.

With Ed back in Omaha, Mary and her mother occasionally drove to Minneapolis to shop. Wender's, just off Nicollet on Seventh, became their favorite store. Wender's stocked petite sizes, an unusual occurrence in 1952. "You'll have to take off a few pounds to fit into that one," Mary teased as Madeline paraded out of the dressing room in an outfit that revealed every one of her 140 pounds.

"Well, you'll have to gain a few to have anything fit that flimsy frame of yours," Madeline retorted. It was their way of having fun.

Madeline enjoyed those outings so much that she often drove her new blue two-door Chevrolet ninety miles to Kensington to pick up her daughter. Otherwise, Mary had to ride to Alexandria with a fellow teacher from Bemidji and then take a bus to St. Cloud. On a Friday afternoon in early December, the two women drove into a blizzard on their way to St. Cloud. It had started as a light snow on Wednesday, which continued through Thursday. Madeline thought the situation a bit iffy but decided not to disappoint her daughter. The trip to Kensington had gone smoothly enough, but, on the return trip, the northwest wind began to whip the snow ferociously across the narrow highway and stack it up on the already high embankments along the shoulders of the road. When Madeline and Mary got as far as Glenwood, Highway 55 had become an open-to-the-sky tunnel. Few cars were on the road, and those that were crawled cautiously along.

"I'm sure we can make it, Mom," Mary encouraged her worried mother. "Just let me drive for a while." When the weary pair finally arrived home late that night, they vowed never to put their lives in jeopardy like that again. That drive in a blizzard became one of those events that popped up in conversation for years to come, and each time Mary's appreciation of her mother grew.

With such diversions, the winter passed, and in March, Mary received an unusually newsy letter informing her that Ed planned to spend the summer in Washington, D.C., working at the Pentagon in the Department of the Army. He would be living with his sister in Arlington, Virginia. He hoped they would be able to spend some time together.

Ed saw Mary almost every night all summer long, coming from the southern extremity of the bus line in Arlington to the northern extremity near the Catholic University, and they began to see each other in a different light. While strolling through the beautiful gardens of the Franciscan Monastery one evening, Ed turned to her and said shyly, "Would you consider marrying me?"

Both stunned and amused, Mary answered, "Is this a proposal?"

"Well, I . . . I . . . think so," he stammered.

"This is all too sudden, Ed. I don't know what to say. Let's talk about it when we get back to Minnesota." She squeezed his hand affectionately, and they continued walking.

When Mary began teaching in the fall, this time in Melrose, Ed started graduate school at the University of Minnesota. They dated on weekends, and their relationship took on new dimensions. Ed even lent Mary his car so she could come home more conveniently on weekends, while he took a bus to Minneapolis. The shy young student began to loosen up, and the teacher became more interested.

Mary spent many hours that school year thinking about why she found herself attracted to this shy young man so dedicated to helping others and solving the world's problems. He was certainly not a playboy, just the opposite — a hard-working, serious-minded student from a poor family, interested in education and making the world a better place. She saw in him a basic goodness and altruism that she had not found in the other young men she had dated. There was magnetism about that inner quality that she found mesmerizing and, actually, he did remind her of her father. Ed was also physically attractive, and they had many interests in common.

Just before Christmas, while returning from a movie, Ed stopped his car at a secluded spot along the Mississippi, a popular lover's lane, and took a small box from his pocket. As he opened it, the contents sparkled in the moonlight. It was a diamond ring, not large or ostentatious, but beautiful, indeed. Taking Mary's hand, he asked, "Will you marry me?"

Without hesitation, she answered, "Yes, Ed, I will."

Then he explained how he had bought the ring with blood money, money he had received for giving his rare O negative blood at the University blood bank. "Poor students can't buy big rocks," he explained, and they both laughed. They hugged and kissed and smiled at each other and then drove home to tell their parents.

Madeline was delighted for her daughter, but she again experienced that hollow, aching feeling of loss: her family was downsizing again.

Chapter Thirteen
Writing Straight with Crooked Lines

WHILE MADELINE'S THREE OLDER CHILDREN WERE moving into adulthood, her two younger daughters, now sixteen and fourteen, were experiencing the traumas of adolescence, both victories and defeats. Maxine, the older of the two, had fallen in love with a young man in her high school class who had a soaring spirit of adventure. He was tall, blond, handsome and completely charming. With his laughing blue eyes, he had captured Maxine's heart—but not Madeline's. As a mother, Madeline had more interest in academic achievement and character, and she doubted that Wayne was serious enough for that. The difference of opinion began to cause frequent disagreements between mother and daughter.

On a late September evening, Maxine mustered the courage to tell her mother about her upcoming date with Wayne. "Wayne has asked me to go to the Homecoming dance with him, Mother—and I'm going!"

In her voice Madeline heard defiance, and Maxine's eyes looked steely. Madeline sipped her coffee before answering, "That's wonderful, dear. Will you need a new dress for the dance? Fandel's has a great sale on now."

Maxine was dumbfounded. "You mean you don't care?"

"I'm glad you have a date for the dance, Maxine. With that winning football team at Cathedral this year, everyone should be out celebrating." With that message of neutrality, the controversy faded.

After Maxine had dated Wayne for several months, Madeline found herself beginning to enjoy Wayne's company. When he visited her daughter, he was cheerful, polite and engaging. He was definitely maturing.

On the day before graduation, Wayne came whistling into the Matthews' kitchen. "Hi, Mom!" he greeted Madeline. "How's the insurance business?" Observing something different about her, he continued, "By the way, that's really a neat new hair-do. If you don't mind my saying so, I like it."

Blushing slightly, Madeline thanked the young man for the compliment and invited him to stay for supper. Sometimes she could see why her daughter was attracted to Wayne: he said all the right things at the right times. No one else had even noticed her new shorter hairstyle.

After graduation from Cathedral, Maxine started her college career at St. Cloud State University. She and Wayne became more serious, and Madeline worried that another of her daughters might sacrifice her education for marriage. She soon realized that her concerns were ill founded, however, when Wayne announced that he was enlisting in the Navy.

For the next four years, Wayne wrote to Maxine from the Great Lakes Naval Training Station in Illinois and from Guantanamo Bay Air Station in Cuba. His letters conveyed a passionate love for her and for his new obsession with flying. "Flying a plane is an intoxicating experience, Max," he wrote. "You feel as if the whole world's your oyster."

It was no great surprise to Maxine that, after four years in the Navy, Wayne signed up for a stint in the U.S. Air Force. He served at Chanute Air Force Base near Danville, Illinois. During his Christmas leave, he and Maxine became engaged, and to Madeline's great chagrin, Maxine did not return to school to finish her senior year. Instead, she followed in her sister's footsteps and found a job teaching in the small Minnesota town of Paynesville, where state licensure was not required.

How well Madeline remembered the announcement of their engagement. In his usual, inimitable way, Wayne had bounded into her kitchen on New Year's morning. "Happy New Year, Mom," he shouted—loud enough to wake everyone. "Did you know that Max and I are getting married in August?"

Madeline spun on her heels to face Wayne, her eyes wide in astonishment. "No, Wayne, she *didn't* tell me. As a matter of fact, she isn't up yet." And then, as the impact of his message hit her, she sputtered, "You're . . . you're what?"

Wayne's eyes danced. "We're getting married in August, Mom. Max can stay on at her school until June and then after the wedding come on to Chanute. I'll have an apartment all set up. We planned the whole thing last night. We even drank our New Year's toast to our future in the U.S. Air Force." Noting her expression of shock, Wayne teased, "Where's that big holiday smile, Mom?"

Madeline smiled in spite of herself. This young man could make a joke out of a sermon and a party out of a funeral. Objecting to the marriage plan would be fruitless, Madeline decided. She wrapped her arms around the young man's shoulders and gave him a motherly hug.

Madeline planned a special dinner party for her daughter's twenty-second birthday. Wayne wrote from Chanute that he would make it home for the party. A few days later, a second letter arrived explaining the details of the flight home. Wayne and his St. Cloud buddy, Bernard Vandre, would meet Cy Manfull and his friend from Osakis at the PX at 7:00 A.M. on Saturday morning. The four of them would drive to the civilian airfield at nearby Danville and rent a plane. Wayne was jubilant about flying again. He hadn't been in the cockpit since late July before enlisting in the Air Force. "Weather permitting, we'll take off about 8:30 A.M. and be home in time for lunch."

Maxine's face glowed with anticipation as she folded the letter and tucked it into her ribbon-bound pack of love letters on her closet shelf.

On Friday afternoon, Maxine locked her classroom in Paynesville and boarded the ubiquitous Greyhound for her trip back to St. Cloud. She needed a weekend of relaxation, a couple of days away from the trials and pranks of her thirty-five first graders. And what a glorious weekend she had planned!

On Friday evening, Madeline prepared Maxine's favorite Friday night supper, and her daughter could smell the tuna casserole the minute she opened the front door. Hearing familiar footsteps, Madeline hurried into the living room, hugged her daughter warmly, placed her nightcase and coat in the front closet, and then just stood there smiling—as if Maxine were the prodigal daughter come home. Madeline had been a widow for eighteen years, since Maxine was four, and the homecoming of any of her children warmed her heart.

"Wayne's father called about an hour ago, dear," Madeline reported. "He's coming over this evening with a little something for your birthday. I have supper almost ready, so you'll be free to spend the time with him." Speaking of supper sent Madeline scurrying back to the kitchen. "Run upstairs and freshen up, dear. By that time, Kathy will be home, and we can eat."

Mr. Collin's visit was short but pleasant. The little something for Maxine's birthday turned out to be a lovely Fostoria candy dish, one to match the elegant Fostoria goblets Maxine had bought from each of her paychecks and which she stored in her bedroom closet next to her love letters. As Ray Collins waved goodbye from the front sidewalk, he shouted, "We'll see you over the weekend, Max. Wayne wrote me that he would be here Saturday noon or bust."

After the visit, Maxine hugged her mother over and over. "Can you believe it, Mom—for my birthday! That's the most precious gift he could give me. Isn't he wonderful?"

"Yes, Wayne is quite wonderful, honey, and a bit impetuous. Flying in a big commercial airliner in the middle of June frightened me, and here Wayne wants to fly home in a small plane in the middle of February."

"He's a good pilot, Mom, and I know he'll be careful," Maxine assured her mother. Nothing was going to cloud her happiness at the thought of having Wayne home with her again, if only for a weekend.

On Saturday morning, Maxine awoke at 6:15 A.M. She had slept fitfully, having dreamed about a frightful little mouse running around her classroom in Paynesville, frightening everyone. She woke still tired but couldn't sleep. After all, Wayne was coming home that day.

Maxine glanced out her bedroom window and saw small, lazy flakes of snow falling aimlessly to the ground. No wind, but the frost ringing the edges of the window-pane indicated how cold it must be outside. She tossed the bed covers over the pillows and stepped into her slippers.

In a pink terry cloth bathrobe, she made her way down the wooden staircase to the Matthews' kitchen. She could smell the aroma of Maxwell coffee brewing, so she knew her mother had gotten up already. As Maxine approached the doorway to the kitchen, Madeline stopped stirring the oatmeal and pulled the pan off the burner.

"Morning, Mom," Maxine began, eyeing the blueberry muffins on the breakfast table.

"Morning, honey," her mother replied, as she left the stove and took her daughter into her arms. "Happy Birthday to my lovely twenty-two-year-old daughter." Extending her arms then and looking into Maxine's eyes, she continued, "I wish your father could be here to see what a beautiful young woman you've become. You were always his favorite, you know."

"Oh, Mom, you always say that." Maxine blushed. "I'm sure Daddy loved all of his children the same. I just looked more like you, so he maybe favored me a little."

Mother and daughter sat down then to an early morning breakfast of oatmeal, bananas, muffins, and coffee. It was one of their favorites. They talked about the day's schedule and the birthday dinner Madeline had planned for the evening. They agreed on sirloin steak and French fries with a tossed salad on the side. Wayne would enjoy that. He would stay that night with his family in Fernwood but would spend most of the weekend with his fiancee.

After breakfast Maxine dressed, parked herself in a comfortable chair near the telephone and picked up *The Bride* magazine she had brought home for preliminary ideas for her wedding. The bride on the cover looked gorgeous in her long, white lace gown embossed with seed pearls and an ethereal looking veil of white tulle.

When Kathy finally got up and came downstairs, Maxine approached her sister at the breakfast table. "It's about time, sleepyhead. Say, how about driving to the St. Cloud airport with me. I want to be there when Wayne arrives. We could leave here about 11:15 A.M., in case he gets in early. I want to surprise him."

"Okay, okay, I'll go," Kathy said. "He'd better not be late though. I have lots of stuff to do today." Kathy bit into her second muffin.

At exactly 11:15 A.M., the two girls backed Madeline's two-tone Chevy from the garage. Light snow continued to fall, but the driveway was passable.

"It's too early to go," Kathy complained, but Maxine thought it was too late.

"What if he gets in early?" she argued.

Kathy shrugged her shoulders. "It must be love," she mumbled and turned the car onto the airport road.

At home, Madeline pushed the heavy upright cleaner behind the davenport as far as it would comfortably go. "No use killing myself over a little dust," she mused. "Besides, Wayne would be the last person on earth to notice." The telephone rang several times before Madeline could make her way across the room.

A little out of breath, she snapped at the caller. "Hello!"

"Hi, Mom! How's my second favorite mother?"

Madeline immediately recognized the familiar voice of Wayne Collins.

"Are you here already? The girls left a few minutes ago for the airport. They'll be so sorry they missed your landing."

"Aw, no! They aren't out there waiting, I hope. I'm sill in Danville, Mom. The weather is lousy here, and visibility is a real problem. We've been trying to get off the ground since 8:30. I'll call Max at the airport and try to explain the situation."

At 4:30 p.m., Maxine arrived home, the figure of gloom. "I guess he couldn't do the impossible," she said, then went straight to her bedroom and spent the rest of the day with an excruciating headache.

After a simple dinner on Sunday, Maxine took the bus back to Paynesville and prepared a lesson for the usual difficult Monday, when the children were always restless, and the teacher, too, needed time to adjust. "Sometimes life is so unfair," she complained as she turned out the light beside her bed.

On Monday morning, Madeline began sorting the wash in her dimly lit basement laundry. She hated the monotony of sorting, washing and then guiding each garment through the wringer of her Maytag. She would rather be filling out insurance applications in her sunlit dining room upstairs or perhaps watching a news report on her new Zenith television. As she dropped her blue polyester slacks onto the colored pile, she observed, "Am I really a size fourteen?" The sound of the telephone interrupted her thoughts, and she started up the basement stairs.

"Hello!" came the voice of a stranger on the other end of the line. "Is Maxine at home?"

"No," Madeline said. "She teaches in Paynesville."

The woman's voice continued. "Well, could you tell me if she saw Wayne Collins over the weekend? Was he there at all?"

"No, he wasn't," Madeline answered emphatically. "He was supposed to fly home on Saturday, but he phoned and said the weather was bad there. Would you like to leave a message for Maxine?"

"No, thank you very much. Goodbye." The voice was gone before Madeline could ask her name.

That's funny, thought Madeline. *I wonder who would be calling Maxine who doesn't know that she teaches in Paynesville. And such a nosey woman, too.* She started back down the steps to her washtubs.

Madeline always had a hamburger with plenty of onions for Monday lunch. It was easy to fix, and no one was there to mind the dubious aroma of onions that swept through the house. She had just sat down to her solitary feast when the telephone rang again. *This is a conspiracy*, thought Madeline, as she reluctantly left her onions.

"Hello, Mrs. Matthews. This is Ray Collins. Did Maxine hear from Wayne any time over the weekend?" The question came with urgency.

"Why, no, she didn't, Mr. Collins—and you're the second person today to ask me that question. Is something wrong?"

"I'm afraid so. The airport called me this morning, saying that they had had a call from Danville, Illinois, requesting information on a plane hired out to Wayne on Saturday with a destination of St. Cloud. The plane never arrived, and now the Civil Air Patrol is conducting a search."

The principal of Paynesville Elementary interrupted Maxine's Monday morning social studies class with an important message. She said there was an urgent call for her in the office. On answering the call, Maxine heard RoseAnn's voice: "Maxine, brace yourself, honey. I hate to tell you this, but Wayne took off in spite of the weather. Now his plane has been reported missing somewhere over Illinois or Wisconsin. The Civil Air Patrol has been out looking for him, but they still don't know what happened."

While listening to her sister's voice, Maxine's whole body began to tremble. She could not believe what she was hearing. Wayne had said he wasn't coming. What could have changed his mind? Then she remembered their conversation and how disappointed she must have sounded. She burst into tears and couldn't find words to answer her sister's message.

Hearing Maxine sobbing and sensing her sister's state of mind, RoseAnn suggested, "Ves and I will come to pick you up, Max. Be ready in an hour. And don't worry, honey, he'll be okay."

A week later, Wayne, the handsome, impetuous young man of Maxine's dreams, was buried on a quiet hillside in Assumption Cemetery about half a mile from his family's home. His Piper Tri-pacer had iced up over Yorkville, Illinois, and crashed. He and his three Air Force buddies died instantly. One of the three was the son of the owner of Van's Flying Service at the St. Cloud airport, which was the destination of the airmen's journey. Civil Air Patrol planes from four states had searched for the missing plane for three days. A farmer and his son finally found the wreckage buried deep in the hollow of a cornfield near

Yorkville about 3:00 Wednesday afternoon. The *Minneapolis Morning Tribune* of March 3, 1955, read: "The wreckage indicated the plane had plummeted straight down, nose first, and hit the ground at full speed."

The shock of Wayne's death devastated Maxine so completely that she was unable to continue her teaching that year. Instead, to escape the site of her grief, she spent three months in Cleveland with her brother Lee, who tried to be brother, father, counselor, and doctor to his grieving sister.

Madeline, for the first time, was not able to help her child, and the experience devastated her, too. She had never understood why God had taken Will in the prime of his life, and now her daughter was going through the same trauma.

The tragedy of Wayne's death changed Madeline's life as well as profoundly changing Maxine's. As the beneficiary of Wayne's insurance, Maxine, his fiancee, received $25,000.00, half of which she gave to Wayne's parents. Much of the remainder she gave to her mother to help with a down payment on a home of her own, the first home Madeline had ever owned in her fifty-eight years. The young man whom Madeline had questioned as a proper suitor for her daughter turned out to be her benefactor, and Madeline pondered the profound words of Paul Claudel: "The Lord writes straight with crooked lines."

Chapter Fourteen
Madeline's Alter Ego

THE YOUNGEST OF MADELINE'S DAUGHTERS, Kathleen, was probably the closest to her mother. However, being the youngest, she missed out on much of the camaraderie enjoyed by the older children in the family. As a result, Kathleen found her greatest childhood enjoyment in her southside neighborhood friends, a whole multitude of them. In many ways, she was the leader of the rambunctious group, organizing doll buggy parades, neighborhood plays, lemonade stand sales, and hopscotch tournaments. Madeline tried to supervise these activities from a distance, but she was taken up with her burgeoning business and was sometimes gone when the little girl needed her. As a result, Kathleen developed an unusual relationship with the mother of her friend Mary, who lived across the street from the Matthews' home.

Mrs. Bue came to Kathleen's assistance whenever Madeline had to work late and no one at home could answer the little girl's questions or soothe her hurt feelings. Mrs. Bue made marvelous sticky caramel rolls and chocolate chip cookies, and she saw the little girl through many scraped knees and festering slivers. Madeline usually heard about Kathleen's experiences second hand and marveled at the child's ingenuity. She was pleased, too, that so many others enjoyed her feisty little entrepreneur.

Seven-year-old Kathleen was not particularly fond of school, especially after Madeline transferred her children to private Catholic schools. The nuns with their long black garbs and coif-pinched faces frightened the child. On one occasion, when Sister Martha pulled Kathleen's long dark braids for not answering correctly, the miserably unhappy second grader ran home after school in tears. "I won't go back, Mom. She's so mean," Kathleen sobbed in her mother's outstretched arms. "Please, Mom, don't make me go back. I want to go to Garfield like all the other kids did. Sister Martha hates me."

Madeline hugged her daughter. "Sister doesn't hate you, dear. She probably just had a bad day and took her problems out on you. You should try to forgive her."

"But, Mother," sobbed Kathy, "yesterday she made Kevin stand in the corner for an hour because he couldn't spell his last name."

Madeline eventually agreed to send Kathleen back to Garfield, and there she learned to love school again, just as her brother and sisters had.

Kathleen willingly followed her siblings to Cathedral for her high school education, however. There she took the prescribed liberal arts classes and, in addition, took Latin and Home Economics—mostly to please her mother who believed that a good mix of the practical and the more esoteric made for a roundly educated person.

The boy who sat in front of Kathleen in Latin class developed a crush on her and showed his affection by turning around periodically to stare at her for minutes on end. "Turn around, Bob. You're making me nervous," Kathleen complained, but to no avail. The beleaguered girl complained to her teacher, Sister Andrew, but the nun seemed to enjoy watching what she thought was a budding romance and did nothing to end the siege. She only smiled at Bob and continued her conjugation of the verb "laborare." Bob eventually became an author and professor at a nearby university, but Kathleen always referred to him as "the Creep."

Kathleen actually had no interest in subjects such as Latin and Home Economics. Her interests centered around basic subjects that would help her to become an effective and admired elementary teacher. "Who cares how the Romans lived and talked or how many calories there are in a slice of bread," Kathleen commented to her mother one evening while setting the table for supper and trying to explain her choice of electives for her senior year. "All I want to do is become a good teacher, Mom. And I won't ever pull braids or rap knuckles. I want to be sensitive to my students' problems and encourage them to like school."

A few years later, while a student at the College of St. Benedict, Kathleen met a fun-loving student from nearby St. Cloud State University. For weeks he had made a nuisance of himself touring back and forth past Madeline's house in his souped up Ford, honking his horn and hoping to catch a glimpse of Kathleen. Madeline forbade her daughter to acknowledge the young man's crude maneuvers, so Dick paid his cousin to arrange a blind date with Kathleen. Persistence paid off. After a delightful evening together, Kathleen agreed to date him again. So it went for two fun-filled years of partying and getting acquainted.

Madeline tried to encourage her daughter to consider some of the more diligent students she had been dating from nearby St. John's University, but Kathleen maintained that Dick was more her type. "I don't like those intellectuals, Mom. They're no fun at all."

Not long after her graduation from St. Ben's, when Kathy was teaching elementary school in a Minneapolis suburb — and trying to be not at all like Sister Martha, Dick asked her to marry him, and Kathleen accepted. When the two of them approached Madeline with the news, both Madeline and her daughter knew that this event marked the end of an era.

Madeline's children had always been the anchor in her life, especially since Will's death, and now her life would change dramatically. But she congratulated the smiling couple and wished them well. Looking ahead and acknowledging Dick's love of music, she quipped, "I'll look forward to some fun-loving little musicians down the road."

"You bet," Dick assured her. "And you can teach them to play "Home on the Range" and "When Irish Eyes Are Smiling."

Dick and Kathy married in June 1960. Two of their daughters resembled Dick in interests and demeanor, especially in their love of music. They often joined their father at holiday times when Dick's gifted piano fingers and his mellow tenor voice entertained the whole family. The middle daughter was more like her mother, well organized, a perfectionist and a born teacher. Good-looking, fun loving and intelligent, they formed an active, versatile family.

Tragedy struck when Dick suffered an aneurysm at age forty-seven. The result of chronic hypertension, it took his life in two short weeks. Kathleen was left a widow at age forty-three, just three years older than Madeline had been when Will died. After that, Kathleen and her mother became an inseparable team, and the younger widow continued to follow in her mother's footsteps in numerous and uncanny ways.

Chapter Fifteen
Coping with the Empty Nest

SOMETIME AFTER KATHLEEN'S WEDDING, Madeline received an interesting phone call from an old friend. His father had run the blacksmith shop in St. Martin where Michael and Rosanna had brought their horses to have them shod and their farm equipment to be repaired. As the oldest son, Frank had inherited the family business, Mauer and Sons. Frank and his wife, Martha, had raised a large family and had become stalwarts of the small community of St. Martin. Martha had passed away, and Frank found himself lonely and depressed. He knew that Madeline had lost Will, so he hoped to rekindle an old friendship when he called her.

"How are you, Madeline?" he inquired. "It's been ages since I've seen you. This is Frank Mauer. I'm going to be in St. Cloud today on business, and I thought I might drop by to visit if you aren't too busy."

Happy to hear from her childhood friend, Madeline invited him for coffee. The visit progressed amicably but awkwardly. Madeline, who knew about Frank's wife and could sense her friend's agenda, cringed when he asked, "Are you seeing anyone these days, Madeline?"

"No, I'm a confirmed old maid now, Frank," she answered, trying to inject a bit of levity into the awkward conversation. "Once was enough for me. How are your children doing?" Madeline continued, attempting to put the conversation on more neutral ground. "I understand Theresa lives in St. Cloud now."

They discussed their children's lives for a few minutes, and then Frank returned to the subject he had come to pursue: "I suppose it gets pretty lonely around here with all of the children gone. How do you fill your days? Mine get pretty empty sometimes."

The definite pattern of his questions made Madeline think of her friend John Grey. She saw no point in indulging in a relationship like that again, so Madeline abruptly changed the course of the conversation again. "I'm terribly sorry, Frank, but I have a very important business appointment coming up shortly, and I'll have to leave. But I want you to know how much I appreciate your stopping by."

Frank left the house knowing that his efforts had been rejected.

After Frank's visit, Madeline realized that she never really intended to marry again. "I'm much too independent now to accommodate a husband," she told her family at their Thanksgiving gathering in 1963. "I've been living alone too long."

The children had been teasing their mother about Frank's visit, but the conversation turned serious when Kathleen suggested that her mother rent out her basement apartment, just to have someone in the house with her. The apartment had not been occupied for some time.

"Well, I suppose I could contact Madison School and find myself a teacher to keep me company on the long winter nights and bring a little noise back into the house," Madeline joked.

"Not a bad idea, Mom," said RoseAnn. "You could make a little money that way, too. You won't be selling insurance and investments forever."

Madeline thought about the idea for several weeks. Then, after Christmas, she began to fix up the apartment. She made white, sheer curtains for the windows, transferred some of her Melmac dishes and a few cooking utensils from the huge collection in her cupboards, and bought three new Revere Ware pots and pans. Next she recarpeted the small living room, had the Frigidaire repaired and bought a new Hotpoint range and a used seventeen-inch Philco television. With the renovation completed, Madeline commented to her neighbor, Mrs. Weller, "I might just move down there myself. It's like a cozy little cottage."

The next day Madeline called the secretary, Mrs. Dobson, at Madison School. Everyone in the neighborhood knew that Mrs. Dobson was well versed on everything about Madison School, including when the principal's new baby was due and which students were still sucking their thumbs. She would be the perfect contact.

"I'm looking for a responsible and friendly young teacher to rent my basement apartment, Mrs. Dobson. Do you know of anyone coming for the fall term who might need a place to live? My house is a convenient two blocks from the school." Mrs. Dobson asked all the appropriate questions and then promised to send over any good prospects.

THE NATIONAL ASSOCIATION
ACCIDENT and HEALTH UNDERWRITERS

hereby confers on

Mrs. Madeline Matthews

Membership in the

LEADING PRODUCERS ROUND TABLE for 1947

This Distinction awarded for Exceptional Sales Accomplishment
during the preceding year

PRESIDENT, National Association Accident and Health Underwriters

CHAIRMAN, Leading Producers Round Table

SECRETARY-TREASURER, Leading Producers Round Table

One of Madeline's many recognition awards. 1947.

Diane Smythe from Pipestone, Minnesota, was Madeline's first tenant. On meeting the vivacious and dynamic young woman, Madeline decided she was just the kind of tenant she wanted for her basement apartment. She had just graduated from St. Benedict's and was applying for a first-grade position at Madison School.

Diane loved the "cozy little cottage" and moved there in the fall of 1964. Madeline was delighted to have this cheerful young woman share her home with her. She routinely brought Diane freshly baked goodies when the exhausted teacher returned home from school and shared the *St. Cloud Daily Times* with her every day. She sometimes even invited Diane to have evening meals with her, and their conversations became satisfying vicarious experiences for Madeline, the wannabe teacher.

Passing the meatloaf to her guest, Madeline inquired, "How did things go today, Diane?"

"I learned a lot about first graders today. You really can't put all of them in the same box. Their age, family background, attention span, and their native intelligence make such a difference," Diane began. "I'm slowly getting to know the children better now, and that helps a lot."

"Do you think the girls at that age are more mature than the boys?" Madeline asked.

"Oh sure! The girls are generally more ready to learn, but I do have one little fellow who outshines everyone. I'm beginning to think he's a genius, and he's so sweet. He knows his alphabet and his numbers, and his vocabulary is phenomenal. His name is Sean."

"Isn't that an unusual name in this locale?" Madeline asked. "Aren't most of the children German or Scandinavian?"

Yes, you're right, Madeline. This little boy's name is Sean Olsen. His mother must have hailed from Killarney." Both women laughed and settled down to the meatloaf.

This kind of conversation occurred many times in the following two years. After that Diane left to marry her hometown sweetheart in Pipestone. Diane was the first of many young teachers who rented the apartment of the gracious widow in the little yellow house two blocks from Madison School. On Madeline's birthday and at holiday times, her mailbox overflowed with heartfelt greetings and reminiscences from her girls, accompanied by wedding pictures and snapshots of new babies. These young women enriched Madeline's life, indeed.

Of course, a woman as work-oriented and independent as Madeline soon found too much leisure detrimental to her physical and mental health. After having retired from her insurance and investment business, she needed a productive pastime to make her life purposeful again. The answer came when an Avon Cosmetics representative rang her doorbell one summer day. After purchasing a night cream and some face powder, Madeline inquired about the possibilities of joining the Avon team.

"The possibilities are limitless, Mrs. Matthews, and you could make so many new friends."

"Am I too old?" Madeline asked, aware that her sixty-seventh birthday would arrive in July.

"Absolutely not," answered the eager sales woman. "You don't look a day over fifty."

Before the lucrative holiday season began, Madeline joined the Avon team and started a whole new career at sixty-seven.

For almost twenty years, until she was eighty-five, Madeline sold Avon cosmetics, jewelry, and miscellaneous clothing items. For most of those years, she was a member of the President's Club and at one point received a special recognition award from the president of Avon. Only when her health began to fail and she had to give her beloved Chevy Malibu to one of her grandsons did she give up this job where she had enjoyed hundreds of friends, a sizable amount of income, and small moments of triumph.

The Matthews children, 1947
Kathy, Maxine, Mary, RoseAnn, and Lee

Chapter Sixteen
The Waning Years

AFTER SHE GAVE UP HER CAR, Madeline began to feel like a prisoner in her own home. Her daughter Maxine in Seattle wrote to her every week with news about the grandchildren, and the three daughters who lived close by tried to fill her life with stimulating and worthwhile activities.

Kathy took her grocery shopping on Saturday mornings and to church on Sundays. She also brought her huge numbers of books from the St. Cloud Library, mostly political biographies and historical novels, which Madeline read voraciously. When Kathy arrived with an armful of books, Madeline's eyes lit up. "Did you get the new Kennedy book for me? I called a while back to have my name put on the waiting list."

"I did. They saved me a copy with large print. You must have an in at the library with all the books I check out. I found another World War II book you might like."

Madeline's love for reading kept her mind alert for many years. With her books, she continued her life-long pursuit of education and became an interesting and versatile conversationalist.

Although her mind remained lucid, Madeline's body began to weaken, so her daughter Mary often took her for short walks to help maintain her physical strength. On these walks, they often discussed politics or current affairs. Madeline was a staunch Democrat, but she did not always agree with President Johnson's foreign policy.

"There are a lot of innocent young men dying over there in Vietnam," she complained to Mary on a Tuesday morning walk. "I think Johnson made a big mistake getting mixed up in that miserable fiasco."

"Lyndon Johnson inherited that war, Mom. He didn't start it, you know," interjected Mary.

"Well, he ought to stop it. Humphrey should speak up a little more, too. I don't think he really supports what they're doing over there," insisted Madeline.

So the conversation went until Madeline had actually walked half a mile. It was wonderful therapy for someone who liked to sit and read for hours.

On Sunday afternoons, Madeline's oldest daughter, RoseAnn, always visited her mother and tidied up any unsightly areas, areas that didn't bother Madeline at all. Rosie also took Madeline shopping at Herberger's or Dayton's whenever she had need of new clothes. Their mother-daughter conversations usually centered on family matters, especially on Kay, RoseAnn's daughter with rheumatoid arthritis.

Kay was a beautiful, blonde, curly-headed girl with the green eyes of her grandmother, who had discovered her illness at age eight when she couldn't kneel with her family at her cousin's church wedding. Doctors had found it difficult to diagnose her condition. Eventually, a new pediatrician from Indiana came to St. Cloud and through multiple blood tests diagnosed the illness. It was considered incurable, and everyone in the family thought of Kay as the family saint for all of the suffering she endured.

Kay was not, however, the only one of Madeline's extended family to experience tragedy. Lee's second son, Tim, one of the six children that Lee and his wife, Rock, had adopted, was accidentally killed by a bus as he rounded a mountain curve on his mo-ped in Sierra Leone, Africa, while serving as a public health worker in the Peace Corps. Tim, a Japanese-American boy with high intelligence and potential, wanted to become a doctor like his father, or a psychologist. He was also one of the many thousands of young students who experimented with marijuana during the Vietnam era and was making an effort to vindicate himself while serving in the Peace Corps.

Diabetes also haunted Madeline's family. First, there was Lee, who diagnosed his own condition while performing blood tests in his laboratory at Western Reserve University. Mary followed some years later, and then her son Mike and Kathy's daughter Lisa were diagnosed with the condition. Madeline always wondered if her biological parents had carried the diabetes gene because no one in Will's relationship had ever suffered from the disease.

Divorce, an even more traumatic event, also caused Madeline concern and worry when her daughter Maxine and her husband ended their twenty-five-year marriage. Despite the blessings of four beautiful children and an enviable Lake Sammamish home, the learned psychologist, the author of a book on divorce, left his family in 1985 and never returned.

Disease, death, and divorce, those sad and surreal scenarios, were gradually transcended by the many joys and successes experienced by Madeline's family. Lee received a vast array of awards for his work in Cystic Fibrosis research and even had his laboratory and a wing of his beloved Babies and Children's Hospital named after him. RoseAnn's daughter Sue received the prestigious Athena Award for outstanding achievement by a woman in business, with skills she perhaps inherited from her grandmother. Numerous college scholarships, citizenship medals, athletic trophies, and advanced degrees received by her productive and dedicated line of offspring were sources of great pride for the grandam of the clan.

Madeline's attitude toward both the joys and the sorrows was reflected in her enduring philosophy: it isn't the event itself that affects your life; it's how you react to the trauma. If you try to maintain some resiliency based on faith, you can always survive. It's all part of the journey. That kind of thinking had guided Madeline all of her life, and it sustained her to the end. But when people questioned her about her longevity, she would only quip, "It was pitching bundles on the Murray farm that made me so tough."

When asked about her success in business, she blamed it all on her family. "I had such wonderful children," she told anyone who would listen to her accolades. Indeed, all of her children had absorbed her interest in teaching and service. Lee held the Gertrude Lee Tucker Chair of Pediatrics at Case Western Reserve Medical School in Cleveland. RoseAnn taught in elementary schools for three years and later returned to work as an educational para-professional. Mary taught high school English for eighteen years, ten of which were spent teaching English to refugee and foreign-exchange students. Maxine taught in the elementary schools in Bloomington, and Kathleen taught in Robbinsdale and at Wilson School in St. Cloud and later also worked as an educational para-professional. Madeline, who wanted so much to become a teacher herself, had sown the seeds of learning and service deeply into all of her children.

Toward the end of her life, the unsung heroes among her twenty-five grandchildren made Madeline's life happy and worry-free as she continued to live in that "little yellow house two blocks from Madison School." They shoveled the snow, cut the grass and watered the roses that grew profusely in amazing shades of yellow, red, white, and coral on the sunny side of her house. Whenever her children, grandchildren, or anyone else came to work or visit, Madeline rewarded them with her prize-winning banana bread or some savory blueberry muffins. Hospitality and gratitude were hallmarks of her relationships.

Chapter Seventeen
The Consummate Teacher

"HE'S HAD A STROKE, MOM, and I couldn't do anything to help him." It was Rock, Lee's wife, the woman who had supported his efforts for almost forty years, who delivered the frightening message. Madeline's brilliant doctor son, who had been a diabetic for over twenty-five years, who had been the pillar of strength for the family after his father's death, was now the patient, not the healer. His condition looked serious. The doctors at Western Reserve University Hospitals worked tirelessly to save this man who was such an important member of their staff. Using extraordinary means, they did save his life, only to see him deteriorate steadily for four years. He never again resumed his position as Director of Babies and Children's Hospital nor was able to use the brilliant mind that had brought him national recognition for his pioneering research in the field of Cystic Fibrosis. Ironically, when he died, one of his cystic fibrosis patients, one he had helped qualify for the priesthood, officiated at his funeral Mass.

When her son died in 1988, some of the spirit drained out of Madeline, though at times she seemed to forget that Lee had died. At ninety-one years old, partially blind, troubled with weakness and fatigue, Madeline's general health deteriorated rapidly. No longer able to live alone, she was assisted by a home health aide hired by the family. Madeline was often offended by the woman's presence in her home and scolded her daughters, "Tell her to leave. I can take care of myself." The truth was, she could not, so the woman stayed and cared for Madeline for over two years.

Madeline faced her final challenge with grace, dignity, and determination. Despite the weakness in her legs, she walked at least a block every day. Mary, who had left her teaching position, often accompanied her and tried to convince her mother of the value of getting outdoors each day. "Every walk we take will add another day to your life, Mama," she repeated, and Madeline would look up at her and smile.

"Mama" had now replaced Madeline's former title "Mom" and the more formal "Mother" used by her children only in times of argument or distress. Somehow Mama seemed a softer, gentler name suited to those softer, gentler years.

Mama made a brave effort to continue her reading, too, using a magnifying glass to enlarge the letters. Books had always been her refuge from loneliness, even on the

Murray farm, and she spent end-less hours trying to continue that pursuit.

Holidays she spent with her family, especially Christmas. On her last Christmas, she made the salad for a group of twenty-five at her daughter Mary's house and wiped every piece of the fine china that Mary's husband Ed washed. Together they made an incomparable team. No one could convince Mama to sit down and rest. Perhaps she knew this was her last chance to participate in the activities she loved most.

Madeline Matthews
93½ years old, December 1990

Madeline's children never lost sight of the sacrifices their mother had made for them. Throughout the years, they had honored her in every possible way—with gifts, flowers, cards, loyalty, and especially their love. Their love and loyalty made her final years, that would otherwise have been lonely and dull, an invigorating and joyful experience. In her last days, they tried to let Madeline know how much they loved her. The

Christmas toast that year went something like this: "Here's to a courageous lady who knows how to live and love and has taught her children that fine art, too."

In early March 1991, as Madeline's four daughters stood at her Calvary Cemetery gravesite, they pondered the values that this remarkable woman had handed down to them: generosity, determination, and implicit faith in God and in oneself. She just never, ever gave up. Somehow, somewhere there had always been a solution to a problem, whether it meant borrowing money, working two jobs or trying something previously considered impossible. She was a risk taker, and her innate faith told her that she could do whatever she put her mind to.

Significantly, too, in all her years of working in a man's world, even before the feminism of the sixties, she always remained a lady — a sensitive, feminine, attractive lady. She was never hard, bitter or unsympathetic. She loved a good laugh and a good cry. When her children brought home straight A report cards, an acceptance to Harvard, an engagement ring, or news of an expected baby, she reacted with tears of joy.

At ninety-three, this dedicated woman submitted herself to the Lord. It was not an easy submission; she still loved life intensely. On hearing of her death, her daughter Mary composed these lines while flying over the Pacific Ocean on her way to the funeral:

Mother,
You formed our lives . . . with your own.
You taught us sensitivity, kindness and loyalty,
How to love and how to serve.

You offered us dreams and ambitions,
Inspiring us along the way.

Always you were there, Mother,
And we will miss you.

Epilogue

MADELINE'S TOMBSTONE READS SIMPLY:

Madeline L. Matthews
Born July 22, 1897
Died March 1, 1991

It might have said:

Here lies that Murray girl
Who accepted the challenges of living
With courage, faith, and independent resolve
And did her very best
From the beginning to the end.